Ruskin Bond was seventeen when he wrote the John Llewellyn Rhys Prize-winning *The Room on the Roof*. Now, more than a hundred short stories, innumerable essays, novels, children's tales and a Sahitya Akademi Award later, the 62-year-old author says he is 'growing old disgracefully'.

This comes as good news to his legion of readers who expect—and get—a steady flow of gleaming fiction and semi-autobiographical stories from this hugely irreverent yet sensitive writer.

Ruskin Bond's Ivy Cottage in Landour, something of a landmark in Mussoorie, is the home he shares with his adopted son and his family, and is from where emerge the books that continue to surprise and delight his readers.

ALSO BY RUSKIN BOND

PENGUIN

Delhi Is Not Far: The Best of Ruskin Bond

Indian Ghost Stories (ed.)

Indian Love Stories (ed.)

Indian Railway Stories (ed.)

Night Train at Deoli

Our Trees Still Grow in Dehra

Rain in the Mountains

Room on the Roof: Vagrants in the Valley

Time Stops at Shamli and Other Stories

VIKING

Ruskin Bond: The Complete Stories & Novels

Rain in the Mountains

PUFFIN

Panther's Moon and Other Stories

Room on the Roof

Strangers in the Night

TWO NOVELLAS

Ruskin Bond

PENGUIN BOOKS

Penguin Books India (P) Ltd., 210, Chiranjiv Towers, 43 Nehru Place,
New Delhi 110 019, India
Penguin Books Ltd., 27 Wrights Lane, London W8 5TZ, UK
Penguin Books USA Inc., 375 Hudson Street, New York,
New York 10014, USA
Penguin Books Australia Ltd., Ringwood, Victoria, Australia
Penguin Books Canada Ltd., 10 Alcorn Avenue, Suite 300, Toronto,
Ontario, MAV 3B2, Canada
Penguin Books (NZ) Ltd., 182-190 Wairau Road, Auckland 10, New Zealand

First published in India by Penguin Books India (P) Ltd. 1996

Typeset in *Garamond* by Surya Computer Services, New Delhi

10 9 8 7 6 5 4 3 2

The author wishes to thank Prita Maitra of Penguin India
for her expert editorial help.

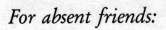

For absent friends:

CONTENTS

ഇരു

ഇരു

CONTENTS

INTRODUCTION

℘℧

Let it be said at the outset that this book is not intended for the school classroom.

Over the years, a number of my stories, some of them written especially for young readers, have found their way into the school or college curriculum, both in India and elsewhere. I have always enjoyed this aspect of my work. But that does not mean I must never write for adults, or that I should refrain from crossing the borderlands of physical passion and human desire. Just now and then I let my hair down and indulge in a little gentle ribaldry or a tale of desire under the deodars.

But you can relax, gentle reader. I am not about to offer you a plateful of porn. *The Sensualist* is the story of a man enslaved by an overpowering sex-drive, but it takes him on the downward spiralling road to self-destruction; you could even say it has a moral.

A Handful of Nuts is about myself at twenty-one, an age that is important to each one of us. It is an age at which we have to come to terms with our own natures if we are to survive the rigours of life's long journey to the end of the night.

Twenty-one was a year of special significance for me. I had published my first book; I was full of hope and ambition, prepared to take chances; and I saw myself as the great lover, as indeed most of us do at that age. I now believe that great lovers are born, not made!

As I grow older, life seems to grow more comical, and I find myself better suited to playing the clown than the romantic hero. At twenty-one, we all aspire to be romantic heroes (or heroines), often with disastrous results. It's an awkward age. You need either money or a beautiful figure to get away with it, and I had neither.

I wrote *A Handful of Nuts* over a period of three-and-a-half months last winter, when icy winds and occasional snowstorms kept me confined to my small abode in the hills. I felt a longing for the hot languorous summer days of my youth, and in this short novel I tried to recapture something of that time and place. Please do not take it as straight autobiography. Some of the people, places and incidents were real; others, creatures of my imagination. It is said that a good story-teller is someone who has a good memory and hopes that other people haven't! I don't think my memory is better than anyone else's, but it is selective, as a writer's must be, and if I have neglected to include some important friends in this novella, it is only because I have saved them up for another tale.

Nor is *The Sensualist* in any way autobiographical. There is a Jekyll and Hyde in each of us, two personalities warring with each other, and to that extent it reveals something of the author's psyche. 'Interesting if true,' said Mark Twain in a different context. 'And if not true, still interesting!'

The Sensualist was written some twenty-two years ago, and first appeared in the Bombay magazine *Debonair*, where it was serialised over three of four issues. One summer's day, while I was enjoying the shade of a maple tree outside my Mussoorie home, a policeman appeared before me with a warrant for my arrest. It was a non-bailable warrant. The policeman was not from the local station. He had come all the way from Bombay to apprehend me. There was an obscenity charge hanging over me in that fair city, and the warrant declared that I was absconding from the law.

That was the time of the Emergency, and writers and journalists were being given a rough time. *Debonair* had just been taken over by Vinod Mehta, and he was greeted with a flurry of prosecutions.

A sympathetic Mussoorie SDM used his discretion and granted me bail, and a couple of months later I took the slow passenger train to Bombay, where I appeared before a very stern and apparently uncompromising judge. The case dragged on for a couple of years, during which I made sporadic appearances, once in order to plead 'Not Guilty'. In the middle of it all, the public prosecutor died of a heart attack. Those who had lodged the complaint which led to the criminal charge of obscenity gradually lost some of their enthusiasm. *Debonair* made a vigorous defence, and writers of the calibre of Nissim Ezekiel and Vijay Tendulkar spoke up for me in court. The judge must have seen some merit in my story, for he gave us all an honourable acquittal. I believe a 60-page judgement reposes in the archives of the Bombay courts.

Nevertheless, I'd been put on the defensive, and I did not publish the story again until about a year ago, when Penguin India decided to include it in the omnibus volume with which they honoured me during their 10th Anniversary celebrations. *Outlook's* literary critic remarks that it unveiled an interesting, complex aspect of this author, and hoped that there would be more in the same vein.

I don't know if *A Handful of Nuts* is in the same vein, but it is certainly another novella, a form that seems to suit my style and temperament. Only the French (and just occasionally the Americans) have really done justice to the short novel. The British prefer the proliferation of the longer novel, and British publishers won't look at a novella; they want their money's worth of words. But the short novel, with its compositional economy and homogeneity of conception, has its place in the scheme of things, as Conrad demonstrated in *Heart of Darkness*, *The Shadow-Line*, *Youth*, and *The Nigger of the Narcissus.* But he was a Pole writing in English.

Although I cannot aspire to being another Conrad, something from the Master may have rubbed off on me, because in *The Sensualist* there is a certain brooding quality and a pessimism which is alien to my nature. I have also used the device of a narrative within a narrative. The recluse in the mountains is my other self, my 'secret sharer'. There is none of that in *A Handful of Nuts,* in which I am my usual irreverent self; it is a self-portrait of the author as a sensitive and occasionally mischievous youth. Or rather, of a mischievous elderly author looking back on his innocent youth!

Ruskin Bond
April, 1996

A Handful
of
Nuts

ONE

ෂ◌ඐ

It wasn't the room on the roof, but it was a large room with a balcony in front and a small verandah at the back. On the first floor of an old shopping complex, still known as Astley Hall, it faced the town's main road, although a walled-in driveway separated it from the street pavement. A neem tree grew in front of the building, and during the early rains, when the neem-pods fell and were crushed underfoot, they gave off a rich, pungent odour which I can never forget.

I had taken the room at the very modest rent of thirty-five rupees a month, payable in advance to the stout Punjabi widow who ran the provisions store downstairs. Her provisions ran to rice, lentils, spices and condiments, but I wasn't doing any cooking then, there wasn't time, so for a quick snack I'd cross the road and consume a couple of samosas or vegetable patties. Whenever I received a decent fee for a story, I'd treat myself to some sliced ham and a loaf of bread, and make myself ham sandwiches. If any of my friends were around, like Jai Shankar or William Matheson, they'd make short work of the ham sandwiches.

I don't think I ever went hungry, but I was certainly underweight and and undernourished, eating irregularly in cheap restaurants and dhabas and suffering frequent stomach upheavals. My four years in England had done nothing to improve my constitution, as there, too, I had lived largely on what was sold over the counter in snack-bars—baked beans on toast being the standard fare.

At the corner of the block, near the Orient Cinema, was a little restaurant called Komal's, run by a rotund Sikh gentleman who seldom left his seat near the window. Here I had a reasonably good lunch of dal, rice and a vegetable curry, for two or three rupees.

There were a few other regulars—a college teacher, a couple of salesmen, and occasionally someone waiting for a film shown to begin. William and Jai did not trail me to this place, as it was a little lowbrow for them (William being Swiss and Jai being Doon School); nor was it frequented much by students or children. It was lower middle-class, really; professional men who were still single and forced to eat in the town. I wasn't bothered by anyone here. And it suited me in other ways, because there was a news-stand close by and I could buy a paper or a magazine and skim through it before or after my meal. Determined as I was to making a living by writing, I had made it my duty to study every English language publication that found its way to Dehra (most of them did), to see which of them published short fiction. A surprisingly large number of magazines did publish short stories; the trouble was, the rates of payment were not very high, the average being about twenty-five rupees a story.

Ten stories a month would therefore fetch me two hundred and fifty rupees—just enough for me to get by!

After eating at Komal's, I made my way to the up-market Indiana for a cup of coffee, which was all I could afford there. Indiana was for the smart set. In the evenings it boasted a three-piece band, and you could dance if you had a partner, although dancing cheek to cheek went out with World War Two. From noon to three, Larry Gomes, a Dehra boy of Goan origin, tinkled on the piano, playing old favourites or new hits.

That spring morning, only one or two tables were occupied—by business people, who weren't listening to music—so Larry went through a couple of old numbers for my benefit, *September Song* and *I'll See You Again*. At twenty, I was very old-fashioned. Larry received three hundred rupees a month and a free lunch, so he was slightly better off than me. Also, his father owned a small music and record shop a short distance away.

While I was sipping my coffee and pondering upon my financial affairs (which were non-existent, as I had no finances), in walked the rich and baggy-eyed Maharani of Magador with her daughter Indu. I stood up to greet her and she gave me a gracious smile.

She knew that some five years previously, when I was in my last year at school, I had been infatuated with her daughter. She had even intercepted one of my love letters, but she had been quite sporting about it, and had told me that I wrote a nice letter. Now she knew that I was writing stories for magazines, and she said, 'We read your story in the *Weekly* last week. It was quite charming, didn't I say you'd make a good writer?' I blushed and thanked her, while Indu gave me a mischievous smile. She was still at college.

'You must come and see us someday,' said the Maharani and moved on majestically. Indu, small-boned and petite and dressed in something blue, looked more than ever like a butterfly; soft, delicate, flitting away just as you thought you could touch her.

They sat at a table in a corner, and I returned to my contemplation of the coffee-stains on the table-cloth. I had, of course, splashed my coffee all over the place.

Larry had observed my confusion, and guessing its cause, now played a very old tune which only Indu's mother would have recognised: *'I kiss your little hands, madame, I long to kiss your lips ...'*

On my way out, Larry caught my eye and winked at me.

'Next time I'll give you a tip,' I said.

'Save it for the waiter,' said Larry.

It was hot in the April sunshine, and I headed for my room, wishing I had a fan.

Stripping to vest and underwear, I lay down on the bed and stared at the ceiling. The ceiling stared back at me. I turned on my side and looked across the balcony, at the leaves of the neem tree. They were absolutely still. There was not even the promise of a breeze.

I dozed off, and dreamt of my princess, her deep dark eyes and the tint of winter moonlight on her cheeks. I dreamt that I was bathing with her in a clear moonlit pool, while small fishes of gold and silver and mother-of-pearl slipped between our thighs. I laved her exquisite little body with the fresh spring water and placed a hibiscus flower between her golden breasts and another behind her ear. I was overcome with lust and threw myself upon her, only to discover that she had turned into a fish with silver scales.

I opened my eyes to find Sitaram, the washerman's son, sitting at the foot of my bed.

Sitaram must have been about sixteen, a skinny boy with large hands, large feet and large ears. He had loose sensual lips. An unprepossessing youth, whom I found irritating in the extreme; but as he lived with his parents in the quarters behind the flat, there was no avoiding him.

'How did you get in here?' I asked brusquely.

'The door was open.'

'That doesn't mean you can walk right in. What do you want?'

'Don't you have any clothes for washing? My father asked.'

'I wash my own clothes.'

'And sheets?' He studied the sheet I was lying on. 'Don't you wash your sheet? It is very dirty.'

'Well, it's the only one I've got. So buzz off.'

But he was already pulling the sheet out from under me. 'I'll wash it for you free. You are a nice man. My mother says you are *seeda-saada*, very innocent.'

'I am not innocent. And I need the sheet.'

'I will bring you another. I will lend it to you free. We get lots of sheets to wash. Yesterday six sheets came from the hospital. Some people were killed in a bus accident.'

'You mean the sheets came from the morgue—they were

used to cover dead bodies? I don't want a sheet from the morgue.'

'But it is very clean. You know *khatmals* can't live on dead bodies. They like fresh blood.'

He went away with my sheet and came back five minutes later with a freshly-pressed bedsheet.

'Don't worry,' he said. 'It's not from the hospital.'

'Where is this one from?'

'Indiana Hotel. I will give them a hospital sheet in exchange.'

❧❦

Two

∞◌∞

The gardens were bathed in moonlight, as I walked down the narrow old roads of Dehra—I stopped near the Maharani's house and looked over the low wall. The lights were still on in some of the rooms. I waited for some time until I saw Indu come to a window. She had a book in her hand, so I guessed she'd been reading. Maybe if I sent her a poem, she'd read it. A poem about a small red virgin rose.

But it wouldn't bring me any money.

I walked back to the bazaar, to the bright lights of the cinemas and small eating houses. It was only eight o'clock. The street was still crowded. Nowadays it's traffic; then it was just full of people. And so you were constantly bumping into people you knew—or did not know ...

I was staring at a poster of Nimmi, sexiest of Indian actresses, when a hand descended on my shoulder, and I turned to see Jai Shankar, the genius from the Doon School, whose father owned the New Empire cinema.

'Jalebis, Ruskin, jalebis,' he crooned. Although he was from a rich family, he never seemed to have any pocket-money. And of course it's easier to borrow from a poor man than it is to borrow from a rich one! Why is that, I wonder? There was William Matheson, for instance, who lived in a posh boarding-house, but was always cadging small sums off me—to pay his laundry bill or assist in his consumption of Charminar cigarettes: without them he was a nervous wreck. And with Jai Shankar it was jalebis ...

'I haven't had a cheque for weeks,' I told him.

'What about the story you were writing for the BBC?'

'Well, I've just sent it to them.'

'And the novel you were writing?'

'I'm still writing it.'

'Jalebis will cost only two rupees.'

'Oh, all right ...'

Jai Shankar stuffed himself with jalebis while I contented myself with a samosa. Jai wished to be an artist, poet and diarist, somewhat in the manner of Andre Gide, and had even given me a copy of Gide's *Fruits of the Earth* in an endeavour to influence me in the same direction. It is still with me today, forty years later, his spidery writing scrawling a message across the dancing angel drawn on the title-page. Our favourite books outlast our dreams ...

Of course, after the jalebis I had to see Jai home. If I hadn't met him, someone else would have had to walk home with him. He was terrified of walking down the narrow lane to his house once darkness had fallen. There were no lights and the overhanging mango, neem and peepal trees made it a place of Stygian gloom. It was said that a woman had hanged herself from a mango tree on this very lane, and Jai was always in a dither lest he should see the lady dangling in front of him.

He kept a small pocket torch handy, but after leaving him at his gate I would have to return sans torch, for nothing could persuade him to part with it. On the way back, I would bump into other pedestrians who would be stumbling along the lane, guided by slivers of moonlight or the pale glimmer from someone's window.

Only the blind man carried a lamp.

'And what need have you of a light?' we asked.

'So that fools do not stumble against me in the dark.'

But I did not care for torchlight. I had taught myself to use whatever the night offered—moonlight, full and partial; starlight; the light from street lamps, from windows, from half-open doors. The night is beautiful, made ugly only by the searing headlights of cars.

When I got back to my room, the shops had closed and only the lights in Sitaram's quarters were on. His parents were quarrelling, and the entire neighbourhood could hear them. It was always like that. The husband was drunk and abusive; she refused to open the door for him, told him to go and sleep with a whore or, better still, a donkey. After some time he retreated into the dark.

I had no lights, as my landlady had neglected to pay the electricity bill for the past six months. But I did not mind the absence of light, although at times I would have liked an electric fan.

It meant, of course, that I could not type or even write by hand except when the full moon poured over the balcony. But I could always manage a few lines of poetry on a large white sheet of paper.

'This sheet of paper is my garden,
These words my flowers.
I do not ask a miracle this night,
Other than you beside me in the bright moonlight.
Naked, entwined like the flowering vine ...'

And there I got stuck. The last lines always fox me, one reason why I shall never be a poet.

'And we cling to each other for a long, long time ...'
Shades of *September Song*?

In any case, I couldn't send it to Indu, as her mother would be sure to intercept the letter and read it first. The idea of her daughter clinging to me like a vine would not have appealed to the Maharani.

I would have to think of a more mundane method of making my feelings known.

THREE

&ca

There was some excitement, as Stewart Granger, the British film actor, was in town.

Stewart Granger in Dehradun? Occasionally, a Bombay film star passed through, but this was the first time we were going to see a foreign star. We all knew what he looked like, of course. The Odeon and Orient Cinemas had been showing British and American films since the days of the silent movies. Occasionally, they still showed 'silents', as their sound systems were antiquated and the projectors rattled a good deal, drowning the dialogue. This did not matter if the star was John Wayne (or even Stewart Granger) as their lines were quite predictable, but it made a difference if you were trying to listen to Nelson Eddy sing *At The Balalaika* or Hope and Crosby exchanging wisecracks.

We had assembled outside the Indiana and were discussing the phenomenon of having Stewart Granger in town. What was he doing here?

'Making a film, I suppose,' I ventured.

Suresh Mathur, the lawyer, demurred, 'What about? Nobody's written a book about Dehra, except you, Ruskin, and no one has read yours. Has someone bought the film rights?'

'No such luck. And besides, the hero is sixteen and Stewart Granger is thirty-six.'

'Doesn't matter. They'll change the story.'

'Not if I can help it.'

William Matheson had another theory.

'He's visiting his old aunt in Rajpur.'

'We never knew he had an aunt in Rajpur.'

'Nor did I. It's just a theory.'

'You and your theories. We'll ask the owner of Indiana. Stewart Granger is going to stay here, isn't he?'

Mr Kapoor of Indiana enlightened us. 'They're location-hunting for a shikar movie. It's called *Harry Black and the Tiger.*'

'Stewart Granger is playing a black man?' asked William.

'No, no, that's an English surname.'

'English is a funny language,' said William, who believed in the superiority of the French tongue.

'We don't have any tigers left in these forests,' I said.

'They'll bring in a circus tiger and let it loose,' said Suresh.

'In the jungle, I hope,' said William. 'Or will they let it loose on Rajpur Road?'

'Preferably in the Town Hall,' said Suresh, who was having some trouble with the municipality over his house tax.

Stewart Granger did not disappoint.

At about two in the afternoon, the hottest part of the day, he arrived in an open Ford convertible, shirtless and vestless. He was in his prime then, in pretty good condition after playing opposite Ava Gardner in *Bhowani Junction*, and everyone remarked on his fine torso and general good looks. He made himself comfortable in a cool corner of the Indiana and proceeded to down several bottles of chilled beer, much to everyone's admiration. Larry Gomes, at the piano, started playing *Sweet Rosie O' Grady* until Granger, who wasn't Irish, stopped him and asked for something more modern. Larry obliged with *Goodnight Irene*, and Stewart, now into his third bottle of beer, began singing the refrain. At the next table, William, Suresh and I, trying to keep pace with the star's consumption of beer, joined in the chorus, and before long there was a mad sing-song in the restaurant.

The editor of the local paper, *The Doon Chronicle*, tried interviewing the star, but made little progress. Someone gave him an information and publicity sheet which did the rounds. It said Stewart Granger was born in 1913, and that he had black hair and brown eyes. He still had them—unless the hair was a toupe. It said his height was 6ft. 2 inches, and that he weighed 196 lbs. He looked every pound of it. It also said his youthful ambition was to become a 'nerve specialist.' We looked at him with renewed respect, although none of us was quite sure what a 'nerve specialist' was supposed to do.

'We just get on your nerves,' said Mr Granger when asked, and everyone laughed.

He tucked into his curry and rice with relish, downed another beer, and returned to his waiting car. A few good-natured jests, a wave and a smile, and the star and his entourage drove off into the foothills.

We heard, later, that they had decided to make the film in Mysore, in distant south India.

No wonder it turned out to be a flop. Sorry, Stewart.

Two months later, Yul Brynner passed through but he didn't cause the same excitement. We were getting used to film stars. His film wasn't made in Dehra, either. They did it in Spain. Another flop.

∞∞

FOUR

ঙ৹ঔ

Why have I chosen to write about the twenty-first year of my life?

Well, for one thing, it's often the most significant year in any young person's life. A time for falling in love; a time to set about making your dreams come true; a time to venture forth, to blaze new trails, take risks, do your own thing, follow your star ... And so it was with me.

I was just back after four years of living in the West; I had found a publisher in London for my first novel; I was looking for fresh fields and new laurels; and I wanted to prove that I could succeed as a writer with my small home town in India as a base, without having to live in London or Paris or New York.

In a couple of weeks' time it would be my twenty-first birthday, and I was feeling good about it.

I had mentioned the date to someone—Suresh Mathur, I think—and before long I was being told by everyone I knew that I would have to celebrate the event in a big way, twenty-one being an age of great significance in a young man's life. To tell the truth I wasn't feeling very youthful. The Komal restaurant's rich food, swimming in oil, was beginning to take its toll, and I spent a lot of time turning input into output, so to speak.

Finding me flat on my back, Sitaram sat down beside me on my bed and expressed his concern for my health. I was too weak to drive him away.

'Just a stomach upset,' I said. 'It will pass off. You can go.'

'I will bring you some curds—very good for the stomach

when you have the *dast*—when you are in full flow.'

'I took some tablets.'

'Medicine no good. Take curds.'

Seeing that he was serious, I gave him two rupees and he went off somewhere and returned after ten minutes with a bowl of curds. I found it quite refreshing, and he promised to bring more that evening. Then he said: 'So you will be twenty-one soon. A big party.'

"How did you know?" I asked, for I certainly hadn't mentioned it to him.

'Sitaram knows everything!'

'How did you find out?'

'I heard them talking in the Indiana, as I collected the table-cloths for washing. Will you have the party in Indiana?'

'No, no, I can't afford it.'

'Have it here then. I will help you.'

'Let's see ...'

'How many people will you call for the tea-party?'

'I don't know. Most of them are demanding beer—it's expensive.'

'Give them *kachi*, they make it in our village behind the police lines. I'll bring a jerry-can for you. It's very cheap and very strong. Big *nasha*!'

'How do you know? Do you drink it?'

'I never drink. My father drinks enough for everyone.'

'Well, I can't give it to my guests.'

'Who will come?'

I gave some consideration to my potential guest list. There'd be Jai Shankar demanding jalebis and beer, a sickening combination! And William Matheson wanting French toast, I supposed. (Was French toast eaten by the French? It seemed very English, somehow.) And Suresh Mathur wanting something stronger than beer. (After two whiskeys, he claimed that he had discovered the fourth dimension.) And there were my young Sikh friends from the Dilaram Bazaar, who would be happy with lots to eat. And perhaps Larry Gomes would drop in.

Dare I invite the Maharani and Indu? Would they fit in with the rest of the mob? Perhaps I could invite them to a separate tea-party at the Indiana. Cream-rolls and cucumber sandwiches.

And where would the money come from for all these celebrations? My bank balance stood at a little over three hundred rupees—enough to pay the rent and the food bill at Komal's and make myself a new pair of trousers. The pair I'd bought on the Mile End Road in London, two years previously, were now very baggy and had a shine on the seat. The other pair, made of non-shrink material, got smaller at every wash; I had given them to a tailor to turn into a pair of shorts.

Sitaram, of course, was willing to lend me any number of trousers provided I wasn't fussy about who the owners were, and gave them back in time for them to be washed and pressed again before being delivered to their rightful owners. I did, on an occasion, borrow a pair made of a nice checked material, and was standing outside the Indiana, chatting to the owner, when I realised that he was staring hard at the trousers.

'I have a pair just like yours,' he remarked.

'It shows you have good taste,' I said, and gave Sitaram an earful when I got back to the flat.

'I can't trust you with other people's trousers!' I shouted. 'Couldn't you have lent me a pair belonging to someone who lives far from here?'

He was genuinely contrite. 'I was looking for the right size,' he said. 'Would you like to try a dhoti? You will look good in a dhoti. Or a lungi. There's a purple lungi here, it belongs to a sub-inspector of police.'

'A purple lungi? The police are human, after all.'

Yes, money talks—and it's usually saying goodbye.

A freelance writer can't tell what he's going to make from

one month to the next. This uncertainty is part of the charm of the writing life, but it can also make for some nail-biting finishes when it comes to paying the rent, the food bill at Komal's, postage on my articles and correspondence, typing paper, toothpaste, socks, shaving soap, candles (there was no light in my room) and other necessities. And friends like William Matheson and Suresh Mathur (the only out-of-work lawyer I have ever known) did not make it any easier for me.

William, though Swiss, had served in the French Foreign Legion, and had been on the run in Vietnam along with the French administration and army once the Vietnamese had decided they'd had enough of the *Marseillaise*. The French are not known for their military prowess, although they would like to think otherwise.

William had drifted into Dehra as the assistant to a German newspaper correspondent, Von Radloff, who based his dispatches on the Indian papers and sent them out with a New Delhi dateline. Dehra was a little cooler than Delhi, and it was still pretty in parts. You could lead a pleasant life there, if you had an income.

William and Radloff fell out, and William decided he'd set up on his own as a correspondent. But there weren't many takers for his articles in Europe, and his debts were mounting. He continued to live in an expensive guest house whose owner, an unusually tolerant landlord, reminded him one day that he was five months in arrears.

William took to turning up at my room around the same time as the postman, to see if I'd received any cheques or international money orders.

'Only pounds,' I told him one day. 'No French or Swiss francs. How could I possibly aspire to a French publisher?'

'Pounds will do. I owe my Sardarji about five thousand rupees.'

'Well, you'll have to keep owing him. My twelve pounds from the *Young Elizabethan* won't do much for you.'

The *Young Elizabethan* was a classy British children's

magazine, edited by Kaye Webb and Pat Campbell. A number of my early stories found a home between its covers. Alas, like many other good things, it vanished a couple of years later. But in that golden year of my debut it was one of my mainstays.

'Why don't you look for cheaper accommodation?' I asked William.

'I have to keep up appearances. How can the correspondent of the Franco-German press live in a hovel like yours?'

'Well, suit yourself,' I said. 'I hope you get some money soon.'

All the same, I lent him two hundred rupees, and of course I never saw it again. Would I have enough for my birthday party? That was now the burning question.

FIVE

৪০০৪

Early one morning I decided I'd take a long cycle ride out of the town's precincts. I'd read all about the dawn coming up like thunder, but had never really got up early enough to witness it. I asked Sitaram to do me a favour and wake me at six. He woke me at five. It was just getting light. As I dressed, the colour of the sky changed from ultramarine to a clear shade of lavender, and then the sun came up gloriously naked.

I had borrowed a cycle from my landlady—it was occasionally used by her son or servant to deliver purchases to favoured customers—and I rode off down the Rajpur Road in a rather wobbly, zig-zag manner, as it was about five years since I had ridden a cycle. I was careful; I did not want to end up a cripple like Denton Welch, the sensitive author of *A Voice in the Clouds*, whose idyllic country cycle-ride had ended in disaster and tragedy.

Dehra's traffic is horrific today, but there was not much of it then, and at six in the morning the roads were deserted. In any case, I was soon out of the town and then I reached the tea-gardens. I stopped at a small wayside teashop for refreshment and while I was about to dip a hard bun in my tea, a familiar shadow fell across the table, and I looked up to see Sitaram grinning at me. I'd forgotten—he too had a cycle.

Dear friend and familiar! I did not know whether to be pleased or angry.

'My cycle is faster than yours,' he said.

'Well, then carry on riding it to Rishikesh. I'll try to keep up with you.'

He laughed. 'You can't escape me that way, writer-sahib.

I'm hungry.'

'Have something, then.'

'We will practise for your birthday.' And he helped himself to a boiled egg, two buns, and a sponge cake that looked as though it had been in the shop for a couple of years. If Sitaram can digest that, I thought, then he's a true survivor.

'Where are you going?' he asked, as I prepared to mount my cycle.

'Anywhere,' I said. 'As far as I feel like going.'

'Come, I will show you roads that you have never seen before.'

Were these prophetic words? Was I to discover new paths and new meanings courtesy of the washerman's son?

'Lead on, light of my life,' I said, and he beamed and set off at a good speed so that I had trouble keeping up with him.

He left the main road, and took a bumpy, dusty path through a bamboo-grove. It was a fairly broad path and we could cycle side by side. It led out of the bamboo grove into an extensive tea-garden, then turned and twisted before petering out beside a small canal.

We rested our cycles against the trunk of a mango tree, and as we did so, a flock of green parrots, disturbed by our presence, flew out from the tree, circling the area and making a good deal of noise. In India, the land of the loudspeaker, even the birds have learnt to shout in order to be heard.

The parrots finally settled on another tree. The mangoes were beginning to form, but many would be bruised by the birds before they could fully ripen.

A kingfisher dived low over the canal and came up with a little gleaming fish.

'Too tiny for us,' I said, 'or we might have caught a few.'

'We'll eat fish tikkas in the bazaar on our way back,' said Sitaram, a pragmatic person.

While Sitaram went exploring the canal banks, I sat down and rested my back against the bole of the mango tree.

A sensation of great peace stole over me. I felt in complete empathy with my surroundings—the gurgle of the canal water, the trees, the parrots, the bark of the tree, the warmth of the sun, the softness of the faint breeze, the caterpillar on the grass near my feet, the grass itself, each blade ... And I knew that if I always remained close to these things, growing things, the natural world, life would come alive for me, and I would be able to write as long as I lived.

Optimism surged through me, and I began singing an old song of Nelson Eddy's, a Vincent Huyman composition—

'When you are down and out,
Lift up your head and shout—
It's going to be a great day!'

Across the canal, moving through some wild babul trees, a dim figure seemed to be approaching. It wasn't the boy, it wasn't a stranger, it was someone I knew. Though he remained dim, I was soon able to recognize my father's face and form.

He stood there, smiling, and the song died on my lips.

But perhaps it was the song that had brought him back for a few seconds. He had always liked Nelson Eddy, collected his records. Where were they now? Where were the songs of old? The past has served us well; we must preserve all that was good in it.

As I stood up and raised my hand in greeting, the figure faded away.

My dear, dear father. How much I had loved him. And I had been only ten when he had been snatched away. Now he had given me a sign that he was still with me, would always be with me ...

There was a great splashing close by, and I looked down to see that Sitaram was in the water. I hadn't even noticed him slip off his clothes and jump into the canal.

He beckoned to me to join him, and after a moment's hesitation, I decided to do so. Sitaram and I romped around in the waist-deep water for quite some time. He was a beautiful glistening chocolate colour in the late morning sunshine. I would have to get into the open more often; I felt pale and washed out.

After some time I climbed the opposite bank and walked to the place where I had seen my father approaching. But there was no sign that anyone had been there. Not even a footprint.

ୟଠ୍ଠ

SIX

 howcs

It was mid-afternoon when we cycled back to the town.
Siesta-time for many, but some brave souls were playing
cricket on a vacant lot. There were spacious bungalows in the
Dalanwala area; they had lawns and well-kept gardens. Dehra's
establishment lived here. As did the Maharani of Magador,
whose name-plate caught my eye as we rode slowly past the
gate. I got off my cycle and stood at the kerb, looking over
the garden wall.

'What are you looking at?' asked Sitaram, dismounting
beside me.

'I want to invite the Maharani's daughter to my birthday
party. But I don't suppose her mother will allow her to
come.'

'Invite the mother too,' said Sitaram.

'Brilliant!' I said. 'Hit two Ranis with one stone.'

'Two birds in hand!' added Sitaram, who remembered his
English proverbs from Class Seven. "And look, there is one
in the bushes!"

He pointed towards a hedge of hibiscus, where Indu was
at work pruning the branches. Our voices had carried across
the garden, and she looked up and stared at us for a few
seconds before recognising me. She walked slowly across the
grass and stopped on the other side of the low wall, smiling
faintly, looking from me to Sitaram and back to me.

'Hello,' she said. 'Where have you been cycling?'

'Oh, all over the place. Across the canal and into the fields
like Hemingway. Now we're on our way home. Sitaram lives
next door to me. When I saw your place, I thought I'd stop

and say hello. Is your mother at home?'

'Yes, she's resting. Do you want to see her?'

'Er, no. Well, sure, but I won't disturb her. What I wanted to say was—if you're free on the 19th, come and join me and my friends for tea. It's my birthday, my twenty-first.'

'How nice. But my mother won't let me go alone.'

'The invitation includes her. If she comes, will you?'

'I'll ask her.'

I looked into her eyes. Deep brown, rather mischievous eyes. Were they responding to my look of gentle adoration? Or were they just amused because I was so self-conscious, so gauche? I could write stories, earn a living, converse with people from all walks of life, ride a bicycle, play football, climb trees, put back a few drinks, walk for miles without tiring, play with babies, charm grandmothers, impress fathers; but when it came to making an impression on the opposite sex, I was sadly out of depth, a complete dunce. It was I, not Indu, who had to hide the blushes ...

Even in London, two years earlier, when I had tried to prove my manhood by going to a prostitute in Leicester Square, everything had gone wrong. She had looked quite attractive under the street light where she had accosted me— or had I accosted her? But when she took me up to her room and exposed her flabby legs and thighs, I was repelled, mainly because she was suffering badly from varicose veins. You linger over your *Playboy* centre-spreads, and then you go out and find your first woman, and she has varicose veins! I gave the unfortunate lady her fee and fled. But the smell of her powder and paint wouldn't leave my coat—my only coat— and I had to live with this failure for days!

The experience convinced me that I was more suited to romantic dalliance than sexual conquests, and that the latter would follow naturally from the former. My intentions towards Indu were perfectly honourable, although I couldn't see her mother accepting me into the royal fold. But perhaps one day when fame and fortune were mine (soon, I hoped!) Indu would give up her protected existence and come and live with me in a house by the sea or a villa on some tropical isle. I made up these lines on the spot, but held back from reciting them:

'With the bougainvillaea in her hair/And blossoms on her breasts/My lips would search between her thighs for honey-dew's caress ...'

As Indu gazed into my eyes, I said, quite boldly and to my own surprise, 'I have to kiss you one of these days, Indu.'

'Why not today?'

She was offering me her cheek, and that's where I started, but then she let me kiss her on her lips, and it was so sweet and intoxicating that when I felt someone pressing my hand I was sure it was Indu. I returned the pressure, then realised that Indu was on the other side of the wall, still holding the hedge-cutters. I'd quite forgotten Sitaram's presence. The pressure of his hand increased; I turned to look at him and he nodded approvingly. Indu had drawn away from the wall just as her mother's voice carried to us across the garden: 'Who are you talking to, Indu? Is it someone we know?'

'Just a college student!' Indu called back, and then, waving, walked slowly in the direction of the verandah. She turned once and said, 'I'll come to the party, mother too!'

And I was left with Sitaram holding my hand.

'Only one thing missing,' he said.

'What's that?'

'*Filmi* music.'

There was *filmi* music in full measure when we got to the Orient Cinema, where they were showing *Mr and Mrs 55* starring Madhubala, who was everybody's heart-throb that year. Sitaram insisted that I return my bicycle and join him in the cheap seats, which I did, almost passing out from the aromatic *beedi* smoke that filled the hall. The Orient had once shown English films, and I remembered seeing an early British comedy, *The Ghost of St. Michael's* (with Will Hay), when I was a boy. The front of the cinema, facing the parade-ground, was decorated with a bas-relief of dancers, designed by Sudhir Khastgir, art master at the Doon School, and they certainly lent character to the building—the rest of its character was fast disintegrating. But I enjoyed watching the crowd at the cinema. For me, the audience was always more interesting than the performers.

All I remember of the film was that Sitaram got very restless whenever Madhubala appeared on the screen. He would whistle along with the tongawallahs and squeeze my arm or other parts of my anatomy to indicate that he was really turned on by his favourite screen heroine. A good thing Madhubala wasn't coming to town, or there'd have been a riot; but for some time there had been a rumour that Prem Nath, a successful male star, would be visiting Dehra, and my landlady had been quite excited at the prospect. But Sitaram was not turned on by Prem Nath. It was Madhubala or nothing.

After the film, while wending our way through the bazaar, we were accosted by Jai Shankar, who walked with us to the Frontier Sweet Shop, where hot fresh jalebis were being dished out to the evening's first customers.

'Your turn to pay,' I said.

'Next time, next time,' promised the pride of the Doon School.

'I'm broke,' I said.

'Your friend must have some money.'

It turned out that Sitaram did possess a few crumpled notes, which he thrust into my hand.

'What does your friend do?' asked Jai.

'He's in the garment business,' I said.

Jai looked at Sitaram with renewed respect. When he'd had his fill of jalebis he insisted on showing us his new painting. So we walked home with him along his haunted alley, and he took us into his studio and proudly displayed a painting of a purple lady, very long in the arms and legs, and somewhat flat-chested.

'Well, what do you think?' asked Jai, standing back and looking at his bizarre creation with an affectionate eye.

'Are you doing it for your school founder's day?' I asked innocently.

'No, nudes aren't permitted. But you should see my study of angels in flight. It won the first prize!'

'Well, if you give this one a halo and wings, it could be an angel'

Jai turned from me in disgust and asked Sitaram for his opinion.

Sitaram stared at the painting quizzically and said, 'She must have given all her clothes for washing.'

'There speaks the garment manufacturer,' I put in.

'The breasts could be bigger,' added Sitaram, as an afterthought.

'Maybe I will enlarge the breasts,' conceded Jai, with a thoughtful nod.

'Not too much,' I said. 'Large breasts are going out of fashion.'

'Why's that?'

'Too many males have them.'

Jai saw us to the door, but not down the dark alley; he never took it alone. All his life he was to be afraid of being alone in the dark. Well, we all have our phobias. To this day, I won't use a lift or escalator unless I have company.

Sitaram and I walked back quite comfortably in the dark. He linked his fingers with mine and broke into song, a little off-key; he was no Saigal or Rafi. We cut across the *maidaan*, and a quarter-moon kept us company. I was overcome by a feeling of tranquillity, a love for all the world, and wondered if it had something to do with the vision of my father earlier in the day.

As we climbed the steps to the landing that separated my

rooms from Sitaram's quarters, we could hear his parents voices raised in their nightly recriminations. His mother was a virago, no doubt; and his father was a drunk who gambled away most of his earnings. For Sitaram it was a trap from which there was only one escape. And he voiced my thought.

'I'll leave home one of these days,' he said.

'Well, tonight you can stay with me.'

I'd said it without any forethought, simply on an impulse. He followed me into my room, without bothering to inform his parents that he was back.

My landlady's large double-bed provided plenty of space for both of us. She hadn't used it since her husband's death, some six or seven years previously. And it was unlikely that she would be using it again.

℠℃

SEVEN

ॐ

Someone was getting married, and the wedding band, brought up on military marches, unwittingly broke into the *Funeral March*. And they played loud enough to wake the dead.

After a medley of Souza marches, they switched to Hindi film tunes, and Sitaram came in, flung his arms around, and shattered my ear-drums with Talat Mehmood's latest love ballad. I responded with the *Volga Boatmen* in my best Nelson Eddy manner, and my landlady came running out of her shop downstairs wanting to know if the washerman had strangled his wife or vice-versa.

Anyway, it was to be a week of celebrations ...

When I opened my eyes next day, it was to find a bright red geranium staring me in the face, accompanied by the aromatic odour of a crushed geranium leaf. Sitaram was thrusting a potted geranium at me and wishing me a happy birthday. I brushed a caterpillar from my pillow and sat up. Wordsworthian though I was in principle, I wasn't prepared for nature red in tooth and claw.

I picked up the caterpillar on its leaf and dropped it outside.

'Come back when you're a butterfly,' I said.

Sitaram had taken his morning bath and looked very fresh and spry. Unfortunately, he had doused his head with some jasmine-scented hair oil, and the room was reeking of it. Already a bee was buzzing around him.

'Thank you for the present,' I said. 'I've always wanted a geranium.'

'I wanted to bring a rose-bush but the pot was too heavy.'

'Never mind. Geraniums do better on verandahs.'

I placed the pot in a sunny corner of the small balcony, and it certainly did something for the place. There's nothing like a red geranium for bringing a balcony to life.

While we were about to plan the day's festivities, a stranger walked through my open door (one day, I'd have to shut it), and declared himself the inventor of a new flush-toilet which, he said, would revolutionise the sanitary habits of the town. We were still living in the thunderbox era, and only the very rich could afford Western-style lavatories. My visitor showed me diagrams of a seat which, he said, combined the best of East and West. You could squat on it, Indian-style, without putting too much strain on your abdominal muscles, and if you used water to wash your bottom, there was a little sprinkler attached which, correctly aimed, would do that job for you. It was comfortable, efficient, safe. Your effluent would be stored in a little tank, which could be detached when full, and emptied—where? He hadn't got around to that problem as yet, but he assured me that his invention had a great future.

'But why are you telling me all this?' I asked, 'I can't afford a fancy toilet-seat.'

'No, no, I don't expect you to buy one.'

'You mean I should demonstrate?'

'Not at all. But you are a writer, I hear. I want a name for my new toilet-seat. Can you help?'

'Why not call it the Sit-Safe?' I suggested.

'The Sit-Safe! How wonderful. Young Mr Bond, let me show my gratitude with a small present.' And he thrust a ten-rupee note into my hand and left the room before I could protest. 'It's definitely my birthday,' I said. 'Complete strangers walk in and give me money.'

'We can see three films with that,' said Sitaram.

'Or buy three bottles of beer,' I said.

But there were no more windfalls that morning, and I had to go to the old Allahabad Bank—where my grandmother had kept her savings until they had dwindled away—and withdraw one hundred rupees.

'Can you tell me my balance?' I asked Mr Jain, the elderly clerk who remembered my maternal grandmother.

'Two hundred and fifty rupees,' he said with a smile. 'Try to save something!'

I emerged into the hot sunshine and stood on the steps of the Bank, where I had stood as a small boy some fifteen years back, waiting for Granny to finish her work—I think she had been the only one in the family to put some money by for a rainy day—but these had been rainy days for her son and daughters and various fickle relatives who were always battening off her. Her own needs were few. She lived in one room of her house, leaving the rest of it for the family to use. When she died, the house was sold so that her children could once more go their impecunious ways.

I had no relatives to support, but here was William Matheson waiting for me under the old peepul tree. His hands were shaking.

'What's wrong?' I asked.

'Haven't had a cigarette for a week. Come on, buy me a packet of Charminar.'

Sitaram went out and bought samosas and jalebis and little cakes with icing made from solidified ghee. I fetched a few bottles of beer, some orangeades and lemonades and a syrupy cold drink called Vimto which was all the rage then. My landlady, hearing that I was throwing a party, sent me pakoras made with green chillies.

The party, when it happened, was something of an anti-climax:

Jai Shankar turned up promptly and ate all the jalebis.

William arrived with Suresh Mathur, finished the beer, and demanded more.

Nobody paid much attention to Sitaram, he seemed so much at home. Caste didn't count for much in a fairly modern town, as Dehra was in those days. In any case, from the way Sitaram was strutting around, acting as though he owned the place, it was generally presumed that he was the landlady's son. He brought up a second relay of the lady's pakoras, hotter than the first lot, and they arrived just as the Maharani and Indu appeared in the doorway.

'Happy birthday, dear boy,' boomed the Maharani and seized the largest chilli pakora. Indu appeared behind her and gave me a box wrapped in gold and silver cellophane. I put it on my desk and hoped it contained chocolates, not studs and a tie-pin.

The chilli pakoras did not take long to violate the Maharani's taste-buds.

'Water, water!' she cried, and seeing the bathroom door open, made a dash for the tap.

Alas, the bathroom was the least attractive aspect of my flat. It had yet to be equipped with anything resembling the newly-invented Sit-Safe. But the lid of the thunderbox was fortunately down, as this particular safe hadn't been emptied for a couple of days. It was crowned by a rusty old tin mug. On the wall hung a towel that had seen better days. The remnants of a cake of Lifebuoy soap stood near a cracked washbasin. A lonely cockroach gave the Maharani a welcoming genuflection.

Taking all this in at a glance, she backed out, holding her hand to her mouth.

'Try a Vimto,' said William, holding out a bottle gone warm and sticky.

'A glass of beer?' asked Jai Shankar.

The Maharani grabbed a glass of beer and swallowed it in one long gulp. She came up gasping, gave me a reproachful look—as though the chilli pakora had been intended for her—and said, 'Must go now. Just stopped by to greet you. Thank you very much—you must come to Indu's birthday party. *Next* year.'

Next year seemed a long way off.

'Thank you for the present,' I said.

And then they were gone, and I was left to entertain my cronies.

Suresh Mathur was demanding something stronger than beer, and as I felt that way myself, we trooped off to the Royal Cafe; all of us, except Sitaram, who had better things to do.

After two rounds of drinks, I'd gone through what remained of my money. And so I left William and Suresh to cadge drinks off one of the latter's clients, while I bid Jai Shankar goodbye on the edge of the parade-ground. As it was still light, I did not have to see him home.

Some workmen were out on the parade-ground, digging holes for tent-pegs.

Two children were discussing the coming attraction.

'The circus is coming!'

'Is it big?'

'It's the biggest! Tigers, elephants, horses, chimpanzees! Tight-rope walkers, acrobats, strong men ...'

'Is there a clown?'

'There has to be a clown. How can you have a circus without a clown?'

I hurried home to tell Sitaram about the circus. It would make a change from the cinema. The room had been tidied up, and the Maharani's present stood on my desk, still in its wrapper.

'Let's see what's inside,' I said, tearing open the packet.

It was a small box of nuts—almonds, pistachios, cashew nuts, along with a few dried figs.

'Just a handful of nuts,' said Sitaram, sampling a fig and screwing up his face.

I tried an almond, found it was bitter and spat it out.

'Must have saved them from her wedding day,' said Sitaram.

'Appropriate in a way,' I said. 'Nuts for a bunch of nuts.'

&)CB

EIGHT

ഇൻ

Lines written on a hot summer's night:

'On hot summer nights I dream
Of you beside me, near a mountain stream
Cool in our bed of ferns we lie,
Lost in our loving, as the world slips by.'

I tried to picture Indu in my arms, the two of us watching the
moon come over the mountains. But her face kept dissolving
and turning into her mother's. This transition from dream to
nightmare kept me from sleeping. Sitaram slept peacefully at
the edge of the bed, immune to the mosquitoes that came in
like squadrons of dive-bombers. It was much too hot for any
body contact, but even then, the sheets were soaked with
perspiration.

Tired of his parents' quarrels, and his father's constant
threat of turning him out if he did not start contributing
towards the family's earnings, Sitaram was practically living
with me. I had been on my own for the past five years and
had grown used to a form of solitary confinement. I don't
think I could have shared my life with an intellectual
companion. William and Jai Shankar were stimulating company
in the Indiana or Royal Cafe, but I doubt if I would have
enjoyed waking up to their argumentative presences first
thing every morning. William disagreed with everything I
wrote or said; I was too sentimental, too whimsical, too
descriptive. He was probably right, but I preferred to write in
the manner that gave me the maximum amount of enjoyment.
There was more give and take with Jai, but I knew he'd be

writing a thousand words to my hundred, and this would have been a little disconcerting to a lazy writer.

Sitaram made no demands on my intellect. He left me to my writing-pad and typewriter. As a physical presence, he was acceptable and grew more interesting by the day. He ran small errands for me, accompanied me on the bicycle-rides which often took us past the Maharani's house. And he took an interest in converting the small balcony into a garden—so much so, that my landlady began complaining that water was seeping through the floor and dripping on to the flour snacks in her ration shop.

The red geranium was joined by a cerise one, and I wondered where it had come from, until I heard the Indiana proprietor complaining that one of his pots was missing.

A potted rose-plant, neglected by Suresh Mathur (who neglected his clients with much the same single-minded carelessness) was appropriated and saved from a slow and lingering death. Subjected to cigarette butts, the remnants of drinks and half-eaten meals, it looked as though it would never produce a rose. So it made the journey from Suresh's verandah to mine without protest from its owner (since he was oblivious of its presence) and under Sitaram's ministrations, soon perked up and put forth new leaves and a bud.

My landlady had thrown out a wounded succulent, and this too found a home on the balcony, along with a sickly asparagus-fern left with me by William.

A plant hospital, no less!

Coming up the steps one evening, I was struck by the sweet smell of *Raat-ki-Rani*, Queen of the Night, and I was puzzled by its presence because I knew there was none growing on our balcony or anywhere else in the vicinity. In front of the building stood a neem tree, and a mango tree, the last survivor of the mango grove that had occupied this area before it was cleared away for a shopping block. There were no shrubs around—they would not have survived the traffic or the press of people. Only potted plants occupied the shop-fronts and verandah-spaces. And yet there was that distinct smell of *Raat-ki-Rani*, growing stronger all the time.

Halfway up the steps, I looked up, and saw my father standing at the top of the steps, in the half-light of a neighbouring window. He was looking at me the way he had done that day near the canal—with affection and a smile playing on his lips—and at first I stood still, surprised by happiness. Then, waves of love and the old companionship sweeping over me, I advanced up the steps; but when I reached the top, the vision faded and I stood there alone, the sweet smell of *Raat-ki-Rani* still with me, but no one else, no sound but the distant shunting of an engine.

This was the second time I'd seen my father, or rather his apparition, and I did not know if it portended anything, or if it was just that he wanted to see me again, was trying to cross the gulf between our different worlds, the worlds of yesterday, today, and tomorrow.

Alone on the balcony, looking down at the badly-lit street, I indulged in a bout of nostalgia, recalling boyhood days when my father was my only companion—in the RAF tent outside Delhi, with the hot winds of May and June swirling outside; then the cool evening walks in Chotta Shimla, on the road to Bishop Cotton School; and earlier, exploring the beach at Jamnagar, picking up and storing away different kinds of sea-shells.

I still had one with me—a smooth round shell which must have belonged to a periwinkle. I put it to my ear and heard the hum of the ocean, the siren song of the sea. I knew that one day I would have to choose between the sea and the mountains, but for the moment it was this little sub-tropical valley, hot and humid, patiently waiting for the monsoon rains ...

The mango trees were sweet with blossom. 'My love is like a red, red rose,' sang Robbie Burns, while John Clare, another poet of the countryside, declared: 'My love is like a bean-field in blossom.' In India, sweethearts used to meet in the mango-groves at blossom time. They don't do that any more. Mango-groves are no longer private places. Better a dark corner of the Indiana, with Larry Gomes playing old melodies on his piano ...

I walked down to A.N. John's saloon for a haircut, but couldn't get anywhere near the entrance. An excited but good-natured crowd had taken up most of the narrow road as well as a resident's front garden.

'What's happening?' I asked a man who was selling candyfloss.

'Dilip Kumar is inside. He's having a haircut.'

Dilip Kumar! The most popular male star of the silver screen!

'But what's he doing in Dehra?' I asked.

The candyfloss-seller looked at me as though I was a cretin. 'I just told you—having a haircut.'

I moved on to where the owner of the bicycle-hire shop was standing. 'What's Dilip Kumar doing in town?' I asked. He shrugged. 'Don't know. Must be something to do with the circus.'

'Is he the ringmaster for the circus?' asked a little boy in a pyjama suit.

'Of course not,' said the pigtailed girl beside him. 'The circus won't be able to pay him enough.'

'Maybe he owns the circus,' said the little boy.

'It belongs to a friend of his,' said a tongawallah with a knowing air. 'He's come for the opening night.'

Whatever the reasons for Dilip Kumar's presence in Dehra, it was agreed by all that he was in A.N. John's, having a haircut. There was only one way out of A.N. John's and that was by the front door. There were a couple of windows on either side, but the crowd had them well covered.

Finally the star emerged; beaming, waving to people, looking very handsome indeed in a white bush shirt and neatly pressed silvery grey trousers. There was a nice open look about him. No histrionics. No impatience to get away.

He was the ordinary guy who'd made good.

Where was Sitaram? Why wasn't my star-struck friend in the crowd? I found him later, watching the circus tents go up, but by then Dilip Kumar was on his way to Delhi. He hadn't come for the circus at all. He'd been visiting his young friend Nandu Jauhar at the Savoy in neighbouring Mussoorie.

৪০৫৩

NINE
ဆာ

The circus opened on time, and the parade-ground became a fairy land of lights and music. This happened only once in every five years when the Great Gemini Circus came to town. This particular circus toured every town, large and small, throughout the length and breadth of India, so naturally it took some time for it to return to scenes of past triumphs; and by the time it did so, some of the acts had changed, younger performers had taken the place of some of the older ones, and a new generation of horses, tigers and elephants were on display. So, in effect, it was a brand new circus in Dehra, with only a few familiar faces in the ring or on the trapeze.

The senior clown was an old-timer who'd been to Dehra before, and he welcomed the audience with a flattering little speech which was cut short when one of the prancing ponies farted full in his face. Was this accident or design? We in the audience couldn't tell, but we laughed all the same.

A circus does bring all kinds of people together under the one tent-top. The popular stands were of course packed, but the more expensive seats were also occupied. I caught sight of Indu and her mother. They were accompanied by someone who looked like the Prince of Purkazi. I looked again, and came to the conclusion that it was indeed the Prince of Purkazi. A pang of jealously assailed me. What was the eligible young prince doing in the company of my princess? Why wasn't he playing cricket for India or the minor counties, or preferably on some distant field in East U.P. where bottles and orange-peels would be showered down on the players? Could the Maharani be scheming to get him married to her daughter? The dreadful thought crossed my mind.

He was handsome, he was becoming famous, he was royalty. And he probably owned race-horses.

But not the ones in the circus-ring. They looked reasonably well-fed, and they were obedient; but they weren't of racing stock. A gentle canter around the ring had them snorting and heaving at the flanks as though they'd just finished running all the way from Meerut, their last stop.

Dear Nergis Dalal was watching them with her eagle eye. She was just starting out on her campaign for the SPCA, with particular reference to circus animals, and she had her notebook and fountain-pen poised and ready for action. Nergis, then in her thirties, had come into prominence after winning a newspaper short story contest, and her articles and middles were now appearing quite regularly in the national press. She knew William Matheson and disapproved of him, for he was known to move around in a pony trap. She knew Suresh Mathur and disapproved of *him*; he had shot his neighbour's Dobermann for howling beneath his window all night. She disapproved of the Indiana owner for serving up partridges at Christmas. And did she disapprove of me? Not yet. But I could sense her looking my way to see if I was enjoying the show. That would have gone against me. So I pretended to look bored; then turned towards her with a resigned look and threw my arms up in the air in a sort of world-weary gesture. 'I'm here for the same reasons as you,' was what it meant, and I must have succeeded, because she gave me a friendly nod. Quite a decent sort, Nergis.

There were several other acquaintances strewn about the audience, including a pale straw-haired boy called Tom Alter, who had managed to secure Dilip Kumar's autograph earlier that day. Tom was the son of American missionaries, but his heart was in Hindi movies and already he was nursing an ambition to be a film star.

William and Jai were absent. They felt the circus was just a little below their intellectual brows. Jai said he had a painting to finish, and William was writing a long article on one of the country's Five-Year Plans—don't ask me which one ... At the time a writer named Khushwant Singh was editing a magazine called *Yojana*, which was all about Five-Year Plans, and he had asked William to do the article. I'd offered the editor an article on punch and its five ingredients— spirit, lemon or lime juice, spice, sugar and rose water—but had been politely turned down. Mr Singh liked his Scotch, but punch was not within the purview of the Five-Year Plan.

To return to the circus ... The trapeze artistes (from Kerala) were very good. The girl on the tight rope (from Andhra) was scintillating in her skin-tight, blue-sequinned costume. The lady lion-tamer (from Tamil Nadu) was daunting, although her lion did look a bit scruffy. The talent seemed to come largely from the south, so that it did not surprise me when the band broke into that lovely Strauss waltz, *Roses of the South*.

The ringmaster came from Bengal. He had a snappy whip, and its sound, as it whistled through the air, was sufficient to command obedience from snarling tigers, prancing ponies, and dancing bears. He did not actually touch anyone with it. The whistle of the whip was sufficient.

Sitaram, who sat beside me looking like Sabu in *The Thief of Baghdad*, was enthralled by all he saw. This was his first circus, and every single act and individual performance had his complete attention. His face was suffused with delighted anticipation. He gasped when the trapeze artistes flew through the air. He laughed at the clown's antics. He sang to the tunes the band played, and he whistled (along with the rowdier sections of the audience) when those alluring southern beauties stood upright on their cantering, wheeling ponies—oh, to be a pony!

'Oh, to be a pony
With a girl upon my rump,
And I'll take you round the ring, my dear,
Without a single bump.'

Not one of my best efforts, but it came to me on the spur of the moment and I said it out loud for the benefit of Sitaram.

'Nice song,' he said. 'I like the one on the second pony. Isn't she beautiful?'

'Stunning,' I agreed. 'I like the sparkle in her eyes.'

'Sparkling eyes are for the poets,' said Sitaram, always bringing me back to earth. 'I like her thighs. Say something about her thighs, poet.'

'Her thighs are like melons—' I began.

'Not melons! I hate melons. They grow all over the *dhobi-ghat.*'

'Sorry, friend. Like half-moons? You like moons?'

'Yes. And her lips?'

'Like rosebuds.'

'Rosebuds. Good. And her breasts?'

'Well, in the frilled costume she's wearing, they look like cabbages.'

Sitaram pinched my thigh, fiercely, so that it hurt. But he wasn't angry. His gaze followed the girl on the pony until she, along with the others in the act, made their exit from the ring.

There were a number of other interesting acts—a dare-devil motor-cyclist riding through a ring of fire, the lady-wrestler taking on a rather somnolent bear, and three tigers forming a sort of pyramid atop a revolving platform—but Sitaram was only half-attentive, his thoughts still being with the beautiful, dark, pink-sequinned girl on her white pony.

On the way home he held my hand and sighed.

'I have to go again tomorrow,' he said. 'You'll lend me the money, won't you? I have to see that girl again.'

ᘏᘒ

TEN

ജ&ഇ

For a couple of weeks Sitaram was busy with the circus, and I did not see much of him. When he wasn't watching the evening performance, he was there in the mornings, hanging round the circus tents, trying to strike up an acquaintance with the ring-hands or minor performers. Most of the artistes and performers were staying in cheap hotels near the railway station. Sitaram appointed himself an unofficial messenger boy, and as he was familiar with every corner of the town, the circus people found him quite useful. He told them where they could get their clothes stitched or repaired, dry-cleaned or laundered; he guided them to the best eating-places, cheap but substantial restaurants such as Komal's or Chacha-da-Hotel (no Indiana or Royal Cafe for the circus crew); posted their letters home; found them barbers and masseurs, brought them newspapers. He was even able to get a copy of the *Madras Mail* for the lady lion-tamer.

Late one night (it must have been after the night show was over) he woke me from a deep dreamless sleep and without any preamble stuffed a laddoo into my mouth. Laddoos are not my favourite sweetmeat, and certainly not in bed at midnight, when the crumbs on the bedsheet were likely to attract an army of ants. While I was still choking on the laddoo, he gave me his good news.

'I've got a job at the circus!'

'What, as assistant to the clown?'

'No, not yet. But the manager likes me. He's made me his office boy. Two hundred rupees a month!'

'Almost as much as I make—but I suppose you'll be

running around at all hours. And have you met the girl you liked—the dark girl or the white pony?'

'I have spoken to her. She smiles whenever she sees me. I have spoken to all the girls. They are very nice—especially the ones from the south.'

'Well, you're luckier than I am with girls.'

'Would you like to meet the lady wrestler?'

'The one who wrestles with the bear every night? After that, would she have any time for mere men?'

'They say she's in love with the ringmaster, Mr Victor. He uses his whip if she gets too rough.'

'I don't want to have anything to do with lady wrestlers, lions, bears or whips. Now let me go to sleep. I have to write a story in the morning. Something romantic.'

'What are you calling it?'

'*The Night Train at Deoli*. Now go to sleep.'

He leant over and gave me a quick sharp bite on the cheek. I yelped.

'What's that supposed to be?' I demanded.

'That's how tigers make love,' he said, and vanished into the night.

The monsoon was only a fortnight away, we were told, and we were all looking forward to some relief from the hot and dusty days of June. Sometimes the nights were even more unbearable, as squadrons of mosquitoes came zooming across the eastern Doon. In those days the eastern Doon was more malarious than the western, probably because it was low-lying in parts and there was more still water in drains and pools. Wild boar and swamp deer abounded.

But it was now mango-time, and this was one of the compensations of summer. I kept a bucket filled with mangoes and dipped into it frequently during the day. So did Jai Shankar, William, Suresh Mathur, and others who came by.

One of my more interesting visitors was a writer called G.V. Desani who had, a few years earlier, written a comic novel called *All About H. Hatterr*. I suspect that the character of Hatterr was based on Desani himself, for he was an eccentric individual who told me that he slept in a coffin.

'Do you carry it around with you?' I asked, over a coffee at Indiana.

'No, hotels won't allow me to bring it into the lobby, let alone my room. Hotel managers have a morbid fear of death, haven't they?'

'A coffin should make a good coffee-table. We'll put it to the owner of the Indiana.'

'Trains are fussy too. You can't have it in your compartment, and in the brake-van it gets smashed. Mine's an expensive mahogany coffin, lined with velvet.'

'I wish you many comfortable years sleeping in it. Do you intend being buried in it too?'

'No, I shall be cremated like any other good Hindu. But I may *will* the coffin to a good Christian friend. Would you like it?'

'I rather fancy being cremated myself. I'm not a very successful Christian. A pagan all my life. Maybe I'll get religious when I'm older.'

Mr Desani then told me that he was nominating his own novel for the Nobel Prize, and would I sign a petition that was to be presented to the Nobel Prize Committee extolling the merits of his book? Gladly, I said; always ready to help a good cause. And did I know of any other authors or patrons of literature who might sign? I told him there was Nergis Dalal; and William Matheson, an eminent Swiss journalist; and old Mrs D' Souza who did a gardening column for *Eve's Weekly*; and Holdsworth at the Doon School—he'd climbed Kamet with Frank Smythe, and had written an account for the journal of the Bombay Natural History Society—and of course there was Jai Shankar who was keeping a diary in the manner of Stendhal; and wasn't Suresh Mathur planning to write a PhD. on P.G. Wodehouse? I gave their names and addresses to the celebrated author, and even added that of the inventor of the Sit-Safe. After all, hadn't he encouraged this young writer by commissioning him to write a brochure for his toilet-seat?

Mr Desani produced his own brochure, with quotes from reviewers and writers who had praised his work. I signed his petition and allowed him to pay for the coffee.

As I walked through the swing doors of the Indiana, Indu and her mother walked in. It was too late for me to turn back. I bowed like the gentleman my grandmother had always wanted me to be, and held the door for them, while they breezed in to the restaurant. Larry Gomes was playing *Smoke Gets In Your Eyes* with a wistful expression.

⣷⣦

ELEVEN
ളⓒൟ

Lady Wart of Worcester, Lady Tryiton and the Earl of Stopwater, the Hon. Robin Crazier, Mr and Mrs Paddy Snott-Noble, the Earl and Countess of Lost Marbles, and General Sir Peter de l'Orange-Peel ...

These were only some of the gracious names that graced the pages of the Doon Club's guest and membership register at the turn of the century, when the town was the favourite retiring place for the English aristocracy. So well did the Club look after its members that most of them remained permanently in Dehra, to be buried in the Chandernagar cemetery just off the Hardwar Road.

My own ancestors were not aristocracy. Dad's father came to India as an 18-year old soldier in a Scots Regiment, a contemporary of Kipling's 'Soldiers Three'—Privates Othenis, Mulvaney and Learoyd. He married an orphaned girl who had been brought up on an indigo plantation at Motihari in Bihar. My maternal grandfather worked in the Indian Railways, as a foreman in the railway workshops at some god-forsaken railway junction in central India. He married a statuesque, strong-willed lady who had also grown up in India. Dad was born in the Shahjahanpur military camp; my mother in Karachi. So although my forebears were, for the most part, European, I was third generation India-born. The expression, 'Anglo-Indian', has come to mean so many things—British settler, Old *Koi-Hai*, Colonel Curry or Captain Chapatti, or simply Eurasian—that I don't use it very often. Indian is good enough for me. I may have relatives scattered around the world, but I have no great interest in meeting them. My feet are firmly planted in Ganges soil.

Grandfather (of the Railways) retired in Dehradun (or Deyrah Dhoon, as it was spelt in the old days), and built a sturdy bungalow on the Old Survey Road. Sadly, it was sold at the time of Independence when most of his children decided to quit the country. After my father's death, my mother married a Punjabi gentleman, and so I stayed on in India, except for that brief sojourn in England and the Channel Islands. I'd come back to Dehra to find that even mother and stepfather had left, but it was still home, and in the cemetery there were several relatives including Grandfather and Great-grandmother. If I sat on their graves, I felt I owned a bit of property. Not a bungalow or even a vegetable patch, but a few feet of well-nourished soil. There were even marigolds flowering at the edges of the graves. And a little blue everlasting that I have always associated with Dehra. It grows in ditches, on vacant plots, in neglected gardens, along footpaths, on the edges of fields, behind lime-kilns, wherever there is a bit of wasteland. Call it a weed if you like, but I have every respect for a plant that will survive the onslaught of brick, cement, petrol fumes, grazing cows and goats, heat and cold (for it flowers almost all the year round), and overflowing sewage. As long as that little flowering weed is still around, there is hope for both man and nature.

A feeling of tranquillity and peace always pervaded my being when I entered the cemetery. Were my long-gone relatives pleased by my presence there? I did not see them in any form, but then, cemeteries are the last place for departed souls to hang around in. Given a chance, they would rather be among the living, near those they cared for or in places where they were happy. I have never been convinced by ghost stories in which the tormented spirit revisits the scene of some ghastly tragedy. Why on earth (or why in heaven) should they want to relive an unpleasant experience?

My maternal grandfather, by my mother's account, was a man with a sly sense of humour who often discomfited his relatives by introducing into their homes odd creatures who refused to go away. Hence the tiny Jharipani bat released into

Aunt Mabel's bedroom, or the hedgehog slipped between his brother Major Clerke's bedsheets. A cousin, Mrs Blanchette, found her house swarming with white rats, while a neighbour received a gift of a parcel of papayas—and in their midst, a bright green and yellow chameleon.

And so, when I was within some fifty to sixty feet of Grandfather's grave, I was not in the least surprised to see a full-grown tiger stretched out on his tombstone, apparently enjoying the shade of the magnolia tree which grew beside it.

Was this a manifestation of the tiger cub he'd kept when I was a child? Did the ghosts of long-dead tigers enjoy visiting old haunts? Live tigers certainly did, and when this one stirred, yawned, and twitched its tail, I decided I wouldn't stay to find out if it was a phantom tiger or a real one.

Beating a hasty retreat to the watchman's quarters near the lych-gate, I noticed that a large, well-fed and very real goat was tethered to one of the old tombstones (Colonel Ponsonby of Her Majesty's Dragoons), and I concluded that the tiger had already spotted it and was simply building up an appetite before lunch.

'There's a tiger on Grandfather's grave,' I called out to the watchman, who was checking out his cabbage patch. (And healthy cabbages they were, too.)

The watchman was a bit deaf and assumed that I was complaining about some member of his family, as they were in the habit of grinding their masalas on the smoother gravestones.

'It's that boy Masood,' he said. 'I'll get after him with a stick.' And picking up his lathi, he made for the grave.

A yell, a roar, and the watchman was back and out of the lych-gate before me.

'Send for the police, sahib,' he shouted. 'It's one of the circus tigers. It must have escaped!'

∞CΣ

TWELVE

ಬಿಂದ

Sincerely hoping that Sitaram had not been in the way of the escaping tiger, I made for the circus tents on the parade-ground. There was no show in progress. It was about noon, and everyone appeared to be resting. If a tiger was missing, no one seemed to be aware of it.

'Where's Sitaram?' I asked one of the hands.

'Helping to wash down the ponies,' he replied.

But he wasn't in the pony enclosure. So I made my way to the rear, where there was a cage housing a lion (looking rather sleepy, after its late-night bout with the lady lion-tamer), another cage housing a tiger (looking ready to bite my head off), and another cage with its door open—empty!

Someone came up behind me, whistling cheerfully. It was Sitaram.

'Do you like the tigers?' he asked.

'There's only one here. There are three in the show, aren't there?'

'Of course, I helped feed them this morning.'

'Well, one of them's gone for a walk. Someone must have unlocked the door. If it's the same tiger I saw in the cemetery, I think it's looking for another meal—or maybe just dessert!'

Sitaram ran back into the tent, yelling for the trainer and the ringmaster. And then, of course, there was commotion. For no one had noticed the tiger slipping away. It must have made off through the bamboo-grove at the edge of the parade-ground, through the Forest Rangers College (well-wooded then), circled the police lines and entered the cemetery. By now it could have been anywhere.

It was, in fact, walking right down the middle of Dehra's main road, causing the first hold-up in traffic since Pandit Nehru's last visit to the town. Mr Nehru would have fancied the notion; he was keen on tigers. But the citizens of Dehra took no chances. They scattered at the noble beast's approach. The Delhi bus came to a grinding halt, while tonga-ponies, never known to move faster than a brisk trot, broke into a gallop that would have done them proud at the Bangalore Races.

The only creature that failed to move was a large bull (the one that someimes blocked the approach to my steps) sitting in the middle of the road, forming a traffic island of its own. It did not move for cars, buses, tongas and trucks. Why budge for a mere tiger?

And the tiger, having been fed on butcher's meat for most of its life, now disdained the living thing (since the bull refused to be stalked) and headed instead for the back entrance to the Indiana's kitchens.

There was a general exodus from the Indiana. William Matheson, who had been regaling his friends with tales of his exploits in the Foreign Legion, did not hang around either; he made for the comparative safety of my flat. Larry Gomes stopped in the middle of playing the *Anniversary Waltz*, and fox-trotted out of the restaurant. The owner of the Indiana rushed into the street and collided with the owner of the Royal Cafe. Both swore at each other in choice Pashtu—they were originally from Peshawar: Swami Aiyar, a Doon School boy with ambitions of being a newspaper correspondent, buttonholed me near my landlady's shop and asked me if I knew Jim Corbett's telephone number in Haldwani.

'But he only shoots man-eaters,' I protested.

'Well, they're saying three people have already been eaten in the bazaar.'

'Ridiculous. No self-respecting tiger would go for a three-course meal.'

'All the same, people are in danger.'

'So, we'll send for Jim Corbett. Aurora of the Green Bookshop should have his number.'

Mr Aurora was better informed than either of us. He told us that Jim Corbett had settled in Kenya several years ago.

Swami looked dismayed. 'I thought he loved India so much that he refused to leave.'

'You're confusing him with Jack Gibson of the Mayo School,' I said.

At this point the tiger came through the swing doors of the Indiana and started crossing the road. Suresh Mathur was driving slowly down Rajpur Road in his 1936 Hillman. He'd been up half the night, drinking and playing cards, and he had a terrible hangover. He was now heading for the Royal Cafe, convinced that only a chilled beer could help him recover. When he saw the tiger, his reflexes—never very good—failed him completely, and he drove his car onto the pavement and into the plate-glass window of Bhai Dhian Singh's Wine and Liquor Shop. Suresh looked quite happy among the broken rum bottles. The heady aroma of XXX Rosa Rum, awash on the shopping verandah, was too much for a couple of old topers, who began to mop up the liquor with their handkerchiefs. Suresh would have done the same had he been conscious.

We carried him into the deserted Indiana and sent for Dr Sharma.

'Nothing much wrong with him,' said the doc, 'but he looks anaemic,' and proceeded to give him an injection of vitamin B_{12}. This was Dr Sharma's favourite remedy for anyone who was ailing. He was a great believer in vitamins.

I don't know if the B_{12} did Suresh any good, but the jab of the needle woke him up, and he looked around, blinked up at me, and said, 'Thought I saw a tiger. Could do with a drink, old boy.'

'I'll stand you a beer,' I said. 'But you'll have to pay the bill at Bhai Dhian's. And your car needs repairs.'

'And this injection costs five rupees,' said Dr Sharma.

'Beer is the same price. I'll stand you one too.'

So we settled down in the Indiana and finished several bottles of beer, Dr Sharma expounding all the time on the miracle of Vitamin B$_{12}$, while Suresh told me that he knew now what it felt like to enter the fourth dimension.

The tiger was soon forgotten, and when I walked back to my room a couple of hours later and found the postman waiting for me with a twenty-five rupee money-order from *Sainik Samachar* (the Armed Forces' weekly magazine), I tipped him five rupees and put the rest aside for a rainy day— which, hopefully, would be the morrow, as monsoon clouds had been advancing from the south.

They say that those with a clear conscience usually sleep well. I have always done a lot of sleeping, especially in the afternoons, and have never been unduly disturbed by pangs of conscience, for I haven't deprived any man of his money, his wife, or his song.

I kicked off my chappals and lay down and allowed my mind to dwell on my favourite Mexican proverb: 'How sweet it is to do nothing, and afterwards to rest!'

I hoped the tiger had found a shady spot for his afternoon siesta. With goodwill towards one and all, I drifted into a deep sleep and woke only in the early evening, to the sound of distant thunder.

ഇൽ

THIRTEEN

ఇంౚ

The tiger padded silently but purposefully past the Dilaram Bazaar, paying no attention to the screaming and shouting of the little gesticulating creatures who fled at his approach. He'd seen them every night at the circus—all in search of excitement, provided there was no risk attached to it!

Walking down from the other end of the Dilaram Road was a tiger of another sort—sub-inspector Sher ('Tiger') Singh, in charge of the local police outpost. 'Tiger Singh' was feeling on the top of the world. His little thana was notorious for beating up suspected criminals, and he'd had a satisfying night supervising the third-degree interrogation of three young suspects in a case of theft. None of them had broken down and confessed, but 'Tiger' had the pleasure (and what was it if not a pleasure, an appeal to his senses?) of kicking one youth senseless, blackening the eyes of another, and fracturing the ankle and shinbone of the third. The damage done, they had been ejected into the street with a warning to keep their noses clean in the future.

These young men could have saved themselves from physical injury had they disbursed a couple of hundred rupees to the sub-inspector and his cohorts, but they were unemployed and without friends of substance; so, beaten and humiliated, they crawled home as best they could. 'Tiger' Singh liked the money he sometimes picked up from suspects and the relatives of petty offenders; but many years in the service had brought out the sadistic side to his nature, and now he took a certain pleasure in seeing noses broken and teeth knocked out. He claimed that he could extract teeth without anaesthesia, and would do the job free for those who could not afford dentists' bills. There were no takers.

Today he strutted along the pavement, twirling his moustaches with one hand and pulling up his trousers with the other. For he was a well-fed gentleman, whose belly protruded above his belt. He had a constant struggle keeping his trousers, along with his heavy revolver holster, from slipping to the ground. Had he not been in the direct path of the tiger, he would have been ignored. But he chose to stand frozen to the ground, really too terrified to reach for his gun or even hitch up his trousers.

The tiger slapped him to the ground, picked him up by his fat neck, and dragged him into the lantana bushes. Sher Singh let out one despairing cry, which turned into a gurgle as the blood spurted from his throat.

The tiger did not eat humans. Their flesh was unappetising, acceptable only to the lame or ageing beasts who could no longer hunt. True, the circus tiger had almost forgotten how to hunt, but his instincts told him that more succulent repasts could be found in the depths of the forest. And the forest was close at hand (or so it was in those days), so he abandoned the dead policeman, who would have made a more suitable meal for vultures had not his colleagues come and taken him away.

The autopsy report said, 'Killed by wild tiger,' which was inaccurate in that the tiger was tame, but it was the only extenuating remark ever made about the sub-inspector. His family received a pension and lived fairly happily ever after.

Neither the tiger nor the S.I. was familiar with the Laws of Karma, or Emerson's Law of Compensation, but they appeared to have been working all the same.

As the tiger sought its freedom in the forest, the clouds that had gathered over the foothills finally gave way under their burden of moisture. The first rain of the monsoon descended upon the hills, the valley, the town. In minutes, a two-month layer of dust was washed away from trees, rooftops and pavements. The rain swept across the streets of Dehra, sending people scattering for shelter. Umbrellas unfolded for the first time in months. A gust of wind shook the circus tent. The old lion, scenting the rain on the wind, sat up in its cage and gave a great roar of delight. The ponies shook their manes, an elephant trumpeted. One of the dwarves, who had been making love to the lady-wrestler, now did so with greater abandon. The ravished lady squealed with pleasure; for it has to be said that the dwarf was undersized in every department but one, and in that one area few could surpass him.

The rain swept over the railway yards, washing the soot and dust from the carriages and engines. It brought freshness and new life to the tea-gardens and sugarcane fields. Even earthworms responded to the cool dampening of their environment and stretched sensuously in the soft mud.

Mud! Buffaloes wallowed in it; children romped in it; frogs broke into antiphonal chants. Glorious, squelchy mud. Hateful for the rest of the year, but wonderfully inviting on the first day of the monsoon. A large amount got washed down from the loose eroded soil of the foothills, so that the streams and canals were soon clogged, silted up, and flooded their banks.

The mango and lichee trees were washed clean. Sal and shisham shook in the wind. Peepal leaves danced. The roots of the banyan drank up the good rain. The neem gave out its heady fragrance. Squirrels ran for shelter into the embracing branches of Krishna's buttercup. Parrots made merry in the guava groves.

I walked home through the rain. Home, did I say? Yes, my small flat was becoming a home, what with Sitaram and his geraniums upstairs, my landlady below, and other familiars in the neighbourhood. Even the geckos on the wall were now recognizable, each acquiring an identity and personality of its own. Sitaram had trained one of them to take food from his fingers. At first he had stuck a bit of meat at the end of a long thin stick. The lizard had snapped up this morsel. Then, every day, he had shortened the stick until the lizard, growing in confidence, took his snack from the short end of the stick and finally from the boy's fingers. I hadn't got around to feeding the wall lizards. One of them had fallen with a plop on my forehead in the middle of the night, and my landlady told me of how a whole family had been poisoned when a gecko had fallen into a cooking pot and been served up with a mixed vegetable curry.

A neighbour, who worked for Madras Coffee House, told me that down south there were a number of omens connected with the fall of the wall lizard, especially if it dropped on some part of your body. He told me that I'd been fortunate that the lizard fell on my forehead, but had it fallen on my tummy I'd have been in for a period of bad luck. But I wasn't taking any chances. The lizards could have all the snacks they wanted from Sitaram, but I wasn't going to encourage any familiarity.

Now, happy to get my clothes wet with the first monsoon shower, I ran up the steps to my rooms, but found them empty. Then Sitaram's voice, raised in song, wafted down to me from the rooftop. I climbed up to the roof by means of an old iron ladder that was always fixed there, and found him on the flat roof, prancing about in the nude.

'Come and join me,' he shouted. 'It is good to dance in the first monsoon shower.'

'You can be seen from the roofs across the road,' I said.

'Never mind. Don't you think I'm the sexiest man of 1955?'

'I shall look forward to seeing you in 1956,' I said, and retreated below.

&?CB

FOURTEEN

୬୯୯ଓ

It was still 1955, and the middle of the monsoon, when Sitaram decided to throw his lot in with the circus and leave Dehra. Those roses of the south had a lot to do with it. I wasn't sure if he was in love with one of the pony-riders, or with the girl on the flying trapeze.

Perhaps both of them; perhaps all of them. He was at an age when his sexual energies had to be directed somewhere, and those beautiful dusky circus girls were certainly more approachable, and more glamorous, than the coy college girls we saw every day.

'So you're going to desert me,' I said, when he told me of his plans.

'Only for a few months. I'll see the country this way.'

'Once with the circus, always with the circus.'

'Well, you have your Indu.'

'I don't. I hear she's getting engaged to that cricket-playing princeling. I hate all cricketers!'

'You're better-looking.'

'But I'm not a prince. I haven't any money, and I don't play cricket. Well, I played a little at school, but they always made me twelfth man, which meant carrying out the drinks like a waiter. What a stupid game!'

'I agree. Football is better.'

'More manly. But not as glamorous.'

Sitaram pondered a while, and then gave me the benefit of his wisdom.

'To win Indu you must win her mother.'

'And how do I do that? She's a dragon.'
'Well, you must pretend you like dragons.'

I was sitting in the Indiana, having my coffee, when Indu's mother walked in. She was alone. (Indu was probably with her prince, learning to bowl under-arm). I said good morning and asked her if she'd like to join me for a cup of coffee. To my surprise, she assented. Larry Gomes was playing *Love is a Many-Splendoured Thing*, and the Maharani was just a bit dreamy-eyed and probably a little sloshed too. But she wasn't in any way attractive. Her eyes were baggy (did she drink?) and her skin was coarse (too many skin lotions?) and her chin was developing a dewlap. Would Indu look like her one day?

She drank her coffee and asked me if I would like a drive. On the assumption that she would be driving me to her house, I thanked her and followed her out of the restaurant, while Larry Gomes looked anxiously at me over his spectacles and broke into the *Funeral March*.

శిౖౘ

FIFTEEN

ഇൻ

Well, it was very nearly my funeral.

Have you ever made love to a dragon—and a scaly one at that? How could a monster like the Maharani have produced a beautiful, tender, vivacious, electrifying girl like Indu? It was like making a succulent dish from a pumpkin, a bitter gourd, and a spent cucumber.

The Maharani had denied me the dish, but she was prepared to give me the ingredients.

She drove me to her home in her smart little Sunbeam-Talbot, and no sooner was I settled on her sofa, with a glass of Carew's Gin in my hand, than I found my free hand encased in a fold of crocodile skin—*her* hand!

A shudder ran down my spine. She mistook the shudder for a shiver of excitement, and started playing with the lobe of my ear. My ear got caught between two of her gold bangles and was almost wrenched off as I jerked my head away. Gin was spilt on my trousers, and I put the glass down on a side-table. As I did so, the Maharani cuddled up to me, and I discovered that the sofa wasn't really large enough for both of us. Also, one was inclined to sink deeper into the upholstery, making a quick escape very difficult.

It had never occured to me that this badly-preserved Christmas pudding could be of an amorous disposition. I had always thought of middle-aged mothers as having gone beyond the pursuit of carnal pleasures. But not this one!

She tried to set me at my ease.

'I'm a child psychologist, you know.'

'But I'm twenty-one.'

'All the better to *treat* you, my dear.'

'Your Highness,' I began.

'Don't Highness me, darling. My pet name is Liz.'

'As in lizard?'

'Cheeky! After Queen Elizabeth.' And she gave me a sharp pinch on the thigh. 'You write poetry, don't you? Recite one of your poems.'

'You need moonlight and roses.'

'I prefer sunshine and cactii.'

'Well, here's a funny one.' I was anxious to please her without succumbing to her blandishments and advances. So I recited my latest limerick.

'There was a fat man in Lucknow
Who swallowed six plates of pillau,
When his belly went bust
(As distended, it must)
His buttons rained down upon Mhow.'

She clapped her hands and shrieked with delight. 'Buttons, buttons!' And she made a grab for mine. (We weren't using zips in those days.)

I tried to get up from the sofa, but she pulled me down again.

'You deserve a reward,' she said, producing a lump of barley-sugar from a box on the side-table. 'This came all the way from Calcutta. Open your mouth.'

Dutifully I opened my mouth. But instead of popping the sweet in, she planted her lips on mine, large lips like suction pumps, and thrust her long lizard-like tongue down my throat. Her crocodile fingers were all over me, and even if my buttons did not reach Mhow, they must have landed on Mussoorie.

What can you do in such a situation? Not much, really.

You just let the more active partner take over—in this case, the rich Maharani of Magador. She certainly knew how to get you worked up. After a hesitant start, all I had to do was imagine that I was another crocodile. I slid into her quivering orifice, and my virginity was at an end.

Afterwards I was rewarded with more barley-sugar and Turkish coffee.

She offered to drop me home, but I said I would walk. Physically I felt great, but I wanted to put my head in order. My thoughts were in whirl. How could I be the Maharani's lover while I was in love with her daughter? Love lyrics for Indu, and limericks for her mother?

'There's no justice anywhere,' I said aloud, in my best William Brown manner. ''T'isn't fair.' And then, as Popeye would have said, 'It's disgustipating!'

And as I closed the gate and stepped onto the sidewalk, who should appear but Indu, riding pillion on her cricketing prince's Triumph motor-bike. At the sight of him my feelings of guilt evaporated. And looking at Indu, smiling insincerely at me, I began to see points of resemblance between her and her mother. Would she be like the Maharani in twenty years' time? I had never seen her father (the late deceased Maharaja of Magador) but fervently hoped that he had been as good-looking as his portraits suggested and that Indu had taken after him.

I gave her and her escort a polite bow (part of my grandmother's influence, no doubt) and set off at a dignified pace in the direction of the bazaar. A car would never be mine, but at least my legs wouldn't atrophy from disuse. Hadn't this very cricketing legend suffered from several torn ligaments in the course of his short career? Chasing cricket balls is a certain way to get a hernia, I said to myself, and then turned my thoughts to the composition of a new limerick in honour of the lady who had just tormented me into becoming her lover. There was no Amnesty International in those days;

I had to defend myself in my own way. So I composed the following lines:

'They called her the Queen of the Nile,
For she walked like a fat crocodile.
But she said, "You young bugger,
I'll make you my *mugger*,"
And took me to bed with a smile.'

৪০৫৩

SIXTEEN

We all need one friend in whom to confide—to whom we can confess our misdemeanours, look for sympathy in times of trouble. Sitaram was my only intimate, and he listened with bated breath while I gave him a hair-raising account of my seduction by royalty. But he wasn't sympathetic. His first response was the following succinct remark:

'Congratulations, *ullu ka pattha.*'

'Why the heady compliment?' I asked.

'Because you cannot escape her now. She'll suck you dry.'

'A succubus, forsooth!'

'Don't use fancy language—you know what I mean. When an older woman gets hold of a young man, she doesn't let him go until he's quite useless to her or anyone else! You'd better join the circus with me.'

'And what do I do in the circus? Feed the animals?'

'They need someone for giving massage.'

'I've always fancied myself as a masseur. Whom do I get to massage—the acrobats, the dancing-girls, the trapeze artistes?'

'The elephants. They lie down and you massage their legs. And backsides.'

'I'll stick to the Maharani,' I said. 'Her skin has the same sort of texture, but there's not so much of it.'

'Well, please yourself ... See, I've brought you a pretty tree. Will you look after it while I'm away?'

It was a red oleander in a pot. It was just coming into flower. We placed it on the balcony beside the rose bush and the geraniums. There were several geraniums now—white, cerise, salmon-pink and bright red—and they were all in flower, making quite a display on the sunny verandah.

'I'll look after them,' I said. 'As long as the landlady doesn't turn me out. The rent is overdue.'

'Don't lend money to your friends. Especially that Swiss fellow. He owes money everywhere—hasn't even paid my parents for two months' washing. One of these days he'll just go away—and your money with him. There is nothing to keep him here.'

'There is nothing to keep *me* here.'

'This is where you belong, where you grew up. You will always be here.'

It was where I had grown up—my mother's, her parents home—but I had always been happier with my father, sharing a wartime tent with him on the outskirts of Delhi or Karachi, visiting the ruins of Old Delhi—Humayun's Tomb, the Purana Killa, the Kashmiri Gate; going to the cinema with him to see the beautiful skating legend, Sonja Henie in *Sun Valley Serenade*; Nelson Eddy singing *Volga Boatmen* and *Ride, Cossack, Ride* in *Balalaika*; Carmen Miranda swinging her hips *Down Argentine Way*; and Hope and Crosby *On the Road to Zanzibar* or *Morocco* or *Singapore*. Rickshaw-rides in Shimla. Ice-creams at Davico's. Comics—*Film Fun* and *Hotspur* ... And those colourful postcards he used to send me once a week. At school, the distribution of the post was always something to look forward to.

But I must also have inherited a great deal of my mother's sensuality, her unconventional attitude to life, her stubborn insistence on doing things that respectable people did not approve of ... Traits that she probably got from her father, a convivial character, who mingled with all and shocked not a few.

I'm sure my mother was quite a handful for my poor father, bookish and intellectual, who did so want her to be a 'lady'. But this was something that went against her nature. She liked to drink and swear a bit. The ladies of the Dehra Benevolent Society did not approve. Nor did they approve of my mother going to church without a hat! This was considered the height of irreverence in those days. There were remonstrances and anguished letters of protest from other (always female) members of the Congregation.

As a result, my mother stopped going to church, and I never picked up the habit. Her sisters, with the exception of the eldest, Enid, were conventional types who found and kept conventional husbands. Aunt Enid, though married to a doctor, distributed her favours on a first-come, first-served basis; she wasn't particular about the cut of your trousers as long as there was something in them. She liked having a good time, and in those war years there was no shortage of Allied troops prepared to make her their mascot. She had a daughter, Sally, who was my age and a bit of a tomboy. Sally and I wrestled in Granny's flowerbeds and took a spirited interest in each other's anatomy. We were only six or seven, and it was all innocent play—or arrested foreplay, I suppose. We sucked each other's lollipops, and this gave us as great a thrill as anything else we did.

Growing up in fairly unfettered fashion, I was quite at ease with Sitaram, another free soul. I was not so sure about the Maharani, although I suspect Aunt Enid would have approved of her. Would she pursue me with relentless abandon, as Sitaram feared, or would she already be looking for other conquests? If she was anything like Aunt E, it would be the latter.

∞∞

SEVENTEEN
∞

The circus tents were being dismantled and the parade-ground was comparatively silent again. Some boys kicked a football around. Others flew kites. The monsoon season is kite-flying time, for it's not too windy, and the moist air-currents are just right for keeping a kite aloft.

In the old part of the Dhamawalla bazaar, there used to be a kite-shop (it was still there five years ago, when I revisited the area), and, taking a circuitous way home, I stopped at the shop and bought a large pink kite. I thought Sitaram would enjoy flying it from the rooftop when he wasn't dancing in the rain. But when I got home, I found he had gone. His parents told me he had left in a hurry, as most of the circus people had taken the afternoon train to Amritsar. He had taken his clothes and a cracked bathroom mirror, nothing else, and yet the flat seemed strangely empty and forlorn without him. The plants on the balcony were poignant reminders of his presence.

I thought of giving the kite to my landlady's son, but I knew him for a destructive brat who'd put his fist through it at the first opportunity, so I hung it on a nail on the bedroom wall, and thought it looked rather splendid there, better than a Picasso although perhaps not in the same class as one of Jai Shankar's angels.

As I stood back, admiring it, there was a loud knocking at my door (as in the knocking at the gate in Macbeth, portending deeds of darkness) and I turned to open it, wondering why I had bothered to close it in the first place (I seldom did), when something about the knocking—its tone, its texture—made me hesitate.

There are knocks of all kinds—hesitant knocks, confident knocks, friendly knocks, good-news knocks, bad-news knocks, tax-collector's knocks (exultant, these!), policemen's knocks (peremptory, business-like), drunkard's knocks (slow and deliberate), the landlady's knock (you could tell she owned the place) and children's knocks (loud thumps halfway down the door).

I had come to recognise different kinds of knocks, but this one was unfamiliar. It was a possessive kind of knock, gloating, sensual, bold and arrogant. I stood a chair on a table, then balanced myself on the chair and peered down through the half-open skylight.

It was Indu's mother. Her perfume nearly knocked me off the chair. Her bosom heaved with passion and expectancy, her eyes glinted like a hyaena's and her crocodile hands were encased in white gloves!

I withdrew quietly and tiptoed back across the room and out on the balcony. On the next balcony, my neighbour's maidservant was hanging out some washing.

'For God's sake,' I told her. 'That woman out front, banging on my door. Go and tell her I'm not at home!'

'Who is she?'

'A *rakshasni*, if you want to know.'

'Then I'm not going near her!'

'All right, can you let me out through your flat? Is there anyone at home?'

'No, but come quickly. Can you climb over the partition?'

The partition did not look as if it would take my weight, so I climbed over the balcony wall and, clinging to it, moved slowly along the ledge till I got to my neighbour's balcony. The maidservant helped me over. Such nice hands she had! How could a working girl have such lovely hands while a lady of royal lineage had crocodile-skin hands? It was the law of compensation, I suppose; Mother Nature looking after her own.

'What's your name?' I whispered, as she led me through

her employer's flat and out to the back stairs.

'Radha,' she said, her smile lighting up the gloom.

'Rather you than that *rakshasni* outside!' I gave her hand a squeeze and said, 'I'll see you again,' then took off down the stairs as though a swarm of bees was after me.

My landlady's son's bicycle was standing in the verandah. I decided to borrow it for a couple of hours.

I rode vigorously until I was out of the town, and then I took a narrow unmetalled road through the sal forest on the Hardwar road. I thought I would be safe there, but it wasn't long before I heard the menacing purr of the Maharani's Sunbeam-Talbot. Looking over my shoulder, I saw it bumping along in a cloud of dust. It was like a chase-scene in a Hitchcock film, and I was Cary Grant about to be machine-gunned from a low-flying aircraft. I saw another narrow trail to the right, and swerved off the road, only to find myself parting company with the bicyle and somersaulting into some lantana bushes. There was a screech of brakes, a car door shot open, and the rich Maharani of Magador was bounding towards me like a man-eating tigress.

'Jim Corbett, where are you?' I called feebly.

'He's in Kenya, you fool,' said the tigress, as she engulfed me and swallowed me whole.

EIGHTEEN
୬୦୧ଔ

A change of air was needed. What with the attentions of the Maharani, the borrowings of William, the loss of Indu, and the absence of Sitaram, I wasn't doing much writing. My bank balance was very low. I had also developed a throat infection, probably as a result of having that rasping lizard's tongue slide down my throat. Anyone else would have bitten it off!

There was the sum of two hundred and seventy rupees in the bank. Always prudent, I withdrew two hundred and fifty and left twenty rupees for my last supper. Then I packed a bag, and left my keys with the landlady with the entreaty that she tell no one in Dehra of my whereabouts, and took the bus to Rishikesh.

Rishikesh was then little more than a village, scattered along the banks of the Ganga where it cut through the foothills. There were a few ashrams and temples, a tiny bazaar, and a police outpost. The saffron-robed sadhus and ascetics outnumbered the rest of the population.

There had been a break in the rains, and I spent a night sleeping on the sands sloping down to the river. The next night it did rain, and I moved to a bench on the small railway platform. I could have stayed in one of the two ashrams, but I had no pretensions to religion of any kind, and was not inclined to become an acolyte to some holy man. Kim had his Lama, the braying Beatles had their Master, and others have had their gurus and godmen, but I have always been stubborn and thick-headed enough to want to remain my own man— just myself, warts and all, singing my own song. Nobody's *chela*, nobody's camp-follower.

Let nature reign, let freedom sing! ...

And, so, on the third morning of my voluntary exile from the fleshpots of Dehra, I strode up river, taking a well-worn path which led to the shrines in the higher mountains. I was not seeking salvation or enlightenment; I wished merely to come to terms with myself and my situation.

Should I stay on in Dehra, or should I strike out for richer pastures—Delhi or Bombay perhaps? Or should I return to London and my desk in the Thomas Cook office? Oh, for the life of a clerk! Or I could give English tuitions, I supposed. Except that everyone seemed to know English. What about French? I'd picked up a French patois in the Channel Islands. It wasn't the real thing, but who would know the difference?

I practised a few lines, reciting aloud to myself:

'*Jeune femme au rendezvous.*
(Waiting for her lover.)
Oh, Oui! Il va venir
(Oh, yes, he is coming!)
Enfin je le verrai!
(Finally I shall see him!)
Pourquoi je attends?
(What am I waiting for?)'

Roll up, folks. Learn how to make love in French! I could see my flat overflowing with students from all over Dehra and beyond. But how was I to keep the Maharani from attending?

The future looked rather empty as I trudged forlornly up the mountain trail. What I really needed just then was a good companion—someone to confide in, someone with whom to share life's little problems. No wonder people get married! An admirable institution, marriage. But who'd marry an indigent writer, with twenty rupees in the bank and no prospects in a land where English was on the way out. (I was not to know that English would be 'in' again, thirty years later.) No self-respecting girl really wants to share the proverbial attic with a down-and-out writer; least of all the princess Indu from Magador. I was pretty sure her mother would let me stay in the garage—but for how long? She was the sort who tired pretty quickly of her playthings.

I should have taken my cricket more seriously, I told myself. Must dress better. Put on the old school tie.

This depressing thought in mind, I found myself standing on the middle of a small wooden bridge that crossed one of the swift mountain streams that fed the great river. No, I wasn't thinking of hurling myself on the rocks below. The thought would have terrified me! I'm the sort who clings to life no matter how strong the temptation is to leave it. But absent-mindedly I leant against the wooden railing of the bridge. The wood was rotten and gave way immediately.

I fell some thirty feet, fortunately into the middle of the stream where the water was fairly deep. I did not strike any rocks. But the current was swift and carried me along with it. I could swim a little (thank God for those two years in the Channel Islands), and as I'd lost my chappals in my fall, I swam and drifted with the current, even though my clothes were an encumbrance. The breast-stroke seemed the best in those turbulent waters, but ahead I saw a greater turbulence and knew I was approaching rapids and, possibly, a waterfall. That would have spelt the end of a promising young writer.

So I tried desperately to reach the river bank on my right. I got my hands on a smooth rock but was pulled away by the current. Then I clutched at the branch of a dead tree that had fallen into the stream. I held fast; but I did not have the strength to pull myself out of the water.

Looking up I saw my father standing on the grassy bank. He was smiling at me in the way he had done that lazy afternoon at the canal. Was he beckoning to me to join him in the next world, or urging me to make a bid to continue for a while in this one?

I made a special effort—yes, I was a stout-hearted boy—

heaved myself out of the water and climbed along the waterlogged tree-trunk until I sank into ferns and soft grass.

I looked up again, but the vision had gone. The air was scented with wild roses and magnolia.

> *'You may break, you may shatter*
> *the vase if you will,*
> *But the scent of the roses will linger*
> *there still.'*

&ℜ&ℭ

NINETEEN
ରେ ଓଡ଼

Back to sleepy Dehra, somnolent in the hot afternoon sun and humid from the recent rain. Dragonflies hovered over the canals. Mosquitoes bred in still waters, multiplying their own species and putting a brake on ours. Someone at the bus stand told me that the Maharani was down with malaria; as a result I walked through the bazaar with a spring in my step, even though my cheap new chappals were cutting into the flesh between my toes. Underfoot, the neem-pods gave out their refreshing though pungent odour. This was home, even though it did not offer fame or riches.

As I approached Astley Hall, I saw a kite flying from the roof of my flat. The landlady's son had probably got hold of it. It darted about, pirouetted, made extravagant nose-dives, recovered and went through teasing little acrobatic sallies, as though it had a life of its own. A pink kite against a turquoise-blue sky.

It was definitely my kite. How dare my landlady presume I had no need for it! I hurried to the stairs, stepping into cow-dung as I went, and consoling myself with the thought that stepping into fresh cow-dung was considered lucky, at least according to Sitaram's mother.

And perhaps it was, because, as I took the narrow stairway to the flat roof, who should I find up there but Sitaram himself, flying my kite without a care in the world.

When he saw me, he tied the kite-string to a chimney-stack and ran up and gave me a tight hug and bit me on the cheek.

'Why aren't you with the circus?' I asked.

'Left the circus,' he said, and we sat down on the parapet and exchanged news.

'What made you leave so suddenly? You were ready to follow those circus-girls wherever they went.'

'They are all in Ambala. There's a big parade-ground there. But it was too hot. Much hotter than Dehra.'

'Is that why you left—because of the heat?'

'Well, there was also this tiger that escaped.'

'But it escaped in Dehra! Don't tell me it returned to the circus?'

'No, no! This was the other tiger. It got out of its cage, somehow.'

'Not again! Did *you* have anything to do with it?'

'Of course not. I hadn't been near it since early that morning.'

'Someone must have left the cage open. Or failed to close it properly.'

'Must have been Mr Victor, the ringmaster. Anyway, when he tried to drive it back into the cage, it sprang on him and took his arm off. He's in hospital.'

'And the tiger?'

'It ran into the sugarcane fields. No one saw it again.'

'So the circus has lost two tigers and the ringmaster his arm. Has the lion escaped too, since you've been there?'

'No, the lion's too old. Besides, it's deeply in love with the lady-wrestler.'

'I thought that was the dwarf.'

'They both love her.'

I gave up. I had a sneaking suspicion that he'd had something to do with the escape of the tiger, but he managed to convince me that he'd come back (a) because of the heat, and (b) because he missed me. In that order. Had it been the other way round, I wouldn't have believed him.

I collected my keys from the landlady (Sitaram had got into the flat through the skylight, anxious to find clues to my whereabouts), and she gave me a couple of letters. One of them contained a cheque from the *Weekly*, with a note from its editor, C.R. Mandy, saying he would be happy to serialize my novel, *The Room on the Roof.* The cheque was for seven hundred rupees.

'We're rich!' I shouted, showing Sitaram the cheque. 'Well, for two or three months, at least ... See, I told you I'd be a successful writer some day!'

'Will there be more cheques?'

'As long as I keep writing.'

'Then sit down and write.' He pulled a chair up for me and forced me to sit in front of my desk.

'Not now, you ass. I'll start tomorrow.'

'No, *today!*'

And so, to make him happy, I wrote a new limerick:

'There was a young fellow called Ram
Who set up a frantic alarm,
For he'd let loose a tiger,
Two bears and a liger,
Who bit off the ringmaster's arm.'

'What's a liger?'

'A cross between a lion and a lady-wrestler.'

'Write more about me.'

'Tomorrow. Now let's go out and celebrate.'

We went to one of the sweetshops near the bazaar and ate jalebis. Jai Shankar found us there and we ate more jalebis.

Then, walking down Rajpur Road, we met William Matheson, who said he was badly in need of a drink. So we took him to the Royal Cafe, where we found Suresh Mathur expounding on the fourth dimension. There were a great many drinks, and everyone got drunk. Suresh Mathur so forgot himself that he signed the chit for the drinks.

It was late evening when we rolled into the Indiana for

dinner. Larry Gomes played *Roll Out The Barrel* and joined us for a beer.

I couldn't write the next day because I had a terrible hangover. But I started again the following day, and I have been writing ever since.

৪৩০৪

EPILOGUE

ഇരുൽ

T he friendly reader knows that I have continued scribbling away for forty years, but he (or she) might well be interested in knowing what happened to the other nuts described in the foregoing pages.

Unlike her mother, Indu grew old quite gracefully. She did not marry the Purkazi prince, as the Maharani had hoped; and this was just as well, for his nose was permanently disfigured by a bump-ball hurled at him by a West Indies paceman. He retired shortly afterward and became a sports journalist known for his bitter diatribes against his fellow cricketers and fast bowlers in particular. Indu married a hotelier in Mauritius where she spends most of her time.

The Maharani of Magador went quite potty in her declining years, took to the bottle, and became convinced that she'd been Mae West in a previous incarnation. Whenever she saw a good-looking man approaching, she welcomed him with the line, 'Is that a gun in your pocket, or are you just happy to see me?'

I met her a few months before she died. She was sitting at the bar of a well-know club in New Delhi, and when I greeted her deferentially, she looked me up and down speculatively and said, 'You're that writer chap, Bunskin Ronde, aren't you? Tried to seduce me when I was a girl!'

William Matheson returned to Switzerland, where he inherited a fortune from his father and lived the good life for a number of years; but he never returned the money he'd borrowed from me.

Suresh Mathur went to practise law in the neighbouring

hill station of Mussoorie, a resort that at close quarters looked as though it had been hammered out of old biscuit-tins. It is prettier at night when darkness hides the scars on its cardboard hillsides. Suresh had one too many Vodka Marys, and finally entered the fourth dimension.

Jai Shankar went to Oxford, where he painted a mural for his college dining-room. Apparently the boat-crew did not like it and dumped him in the Thames near Tilbury. He gave up art when one of his models sued him for exhibiting a painting in which he had shown her with three breasts. He now lives in Paris and writes poems in French.

And what of dear Sitaram?

No, he did not enter his father's profession. He remained with me for another year, and then, at the age of eighteen, decided to try his luck in Mumbai, then Bombay. He went to work for a well-known actress, who liked his winning ways and got him a small part in one of her films. After that, he went from strength to strength and by the time he was in his thirties he was one of the most popular stars of the Indian screen. He wrote to me a couple of times and asked me to come and stay with him; but I felt shy of his success and stayed away. The bright lights, whether in the circus or on the film-sets, were not for me. The writer's art is a lonely one.

Of course Sitaram became famous under another, assumed name, and I am sure, dear reader, that you would like to know his identity. But I have promised to keep it a secret, and so we must leave it at that. But I'll give you a few clues: he doesn't sing, though he dances; he can't act but he has a sexy smile; and although the hair on his head is jet-black, the hair on his torso is now quite grey. But most of them are a bit like that, aren't they?

ළල

The Sensualist

A Cautionary Tale

ONE

৪৩

'When you hold him in your two hands, you should first honour
him duly and then devour him. You will find him with flesh
upon his bones, but leave him as the remnants of a fish, which are
spines and skin. But what am I saying? Even when there is no
flesh left, you shall by no means cast the bones aside till you have
cracked them and sucked the marrow. He must be left incapable
of work, unable even to stumble, with wandering glances, emptied,
broken, finished ...'

Damodaragupta, The Lessons of a Bawd,
(8th century A.D.)

This range is bare and rocky, with steep hillsides suddenly
rearing up in front of the tired, discouraged traveller. The
grass is short and almost colourless. An eagle circles high
overhead and the burning sun, striking through the rarefied
atmosphere, is reflected from the granite rocks. Waves of
banded light shimmer along the dusty mountain path. I walk
alone and I am thirsty.

The last stream disappeared into the valley ten miles back,
and this region seems to be devoid of any kind of moisture.
The villages, the terraced fields, have been left behind. The

pine forests are a purple blanket on the next mountain. I have a long way to go to reach the river and the town. I must have taken the wrong path sometime back, but this doesn't worry me very much. I have lost my way in the hills before and found it again simply by following the line of a valley; but I will not reach the river tonight. It is already half-past three and the September sun is low in the sky.

I have a strong desire to sit down and rest but there is no shade anywhere except under the big boulders which look as though they might topple over at any moment. Huge lizards bask on the rocks, scuttling away at my approach. Where do they get their moisture? Some subterranean pocket of wather must exist here to sustain these creatures, because except for the eagle, I find no other sign of life.

But this path must lead somewhere. There are no mule-tracks, no imprint of human feet to give me confidence, but no mountain path can exist without someone to wear down the sharp rocks and prevent the grass from growing. Someone, at some time, must pass this way, and beyond the next hill there should be a village and grass that is green; perhaps a lime tree with a patch of fragrant shade and a glass of sour curds and a draw at the hookah.

Even while I dream of it, I find a patch of emerald grass at my feet, and trickling through it a sliver of clear water. It comes from a rock in the hillside. Just below the rock the water runs into a small pool made by the human hand, and it is the overflow from this that runs across the path. I drink from the little pool and find the water cool and sweet. I splash my face and let the water run down my neck and arms. Then, looking up, I notice a cave high up on the hillside, with the narrowest of paths leading up to it. There will be shade there and a place to rest.

I clamber up the steep path. The dazzling sun leaps on me like a beast of prey, but I climb higher with the aid of rocks and tufts of grass. The sky turns round and round. Never has it looked so blue

There is someone squatting, crouching at the entrance to the cave. As the sun is in my eyes, I cannot be sure if the creature is human or animal. It doesn't move. It is black and almost formless.

But as I come nearer, it takes the shape of a man.

He is naked except for a tightly wound loincloth. Long, matted hair falls below his shoulders. The ribs show through his chest. His skin has been burnt black by the sun and toughened into old leather by the dry wind that sweeps across the mountains. The eyes are bright black pinpoints in a cavernous face.

'It is some time since I had a visitor.' His voice is deep, sonorous.

I stare at this creature who looks like primitive man but speaks like an angel.

'I lost my way,' I explain.

'I had intended that you should. In a moment of weakness I felt a need for human company, and sent my thoughts abroad to confuse the mind of the first traveller who rounded the bend of the next mountain!'

'I was certainly confused. I hope you will be able to set me on the right path again.'

'All in good time. Will you not sit down here in the shade? I assure you that I am perfectly harmless. I am not even an eccentric, as you might think. For that matter, I am not even lonely. It was just a whim that made me desire your company. I hope you don't mind?'

'No.'

I do not know what to make of him as yet. Here is a

recluse who has obviously spent a long time far from the haunts of men. I do not expect him to think or speak like other men. I realize that my norm is not his, and that, living entirely within himself, he must have attained dimensions of thought that are beyond my reach. The question that troubles me is, 'Can he harm me physically?' I am not afraid of the power of his thoughts, for I have confidence in my own.

He sits in the dust, and as there is no sign of anything resembling a comfortable seat, I drop to the ground, some five feet away from him. It is hot sitting there in the sun, but the only shade is inside the cave, and I do not feel inclined to enter that place. Besides, it will soon be evening and it will be cooler.

&so;&cx;

Two

෨෬

The recluse looks at me, sizing me up, and I recognize the eyes of one with hypnotic gifts. I look away from him, although I know that it is not necessary for him to look at me in order to enter my mind. This is purely a defensive reaction on my part. I can feel the weight of his consciousness and I am immediately aware that he bears no hostility towards me. No action or word of his can make me feel easier than the aura of hopelessness that emanates from his mind, communicating itself to me.

'I suppose you practise many austerities,' I say. 'I admire men who can withdraw from the world, from a life of the senses. But I am not sure that I would want to do the same.'

'You haven't had enough of the senses, perhaps.'

'Did you have too much?'

'Yes, but that was not the only reason ...' He gives me an enigmatic half-smile and I wonder, how long has he been here, and how old is he? It is impossible to tell from his appearance. He might have been here five years or an eternity.

'Perhaps you are hungry?' he asks.

'No. I ate at noon. I was very thirsty, but the spring at the bottom of the hill quenched my thirst. What do you get to eat here?'

'I eat very little. My existence is not entirely supernatural—not yet, anyway—and I must sustain this body of mine a little longer. But I have managed to destroy my former interest in food, and my body gets along quite well on the nourishment it receives. It is a question of conditioning, I suppose.'

'At some stage in your life you received formal education,' I observe.

'Oh yes, a fairly good education, although I never completed a single course. The learning I acquired has made it all the more difficult for me to accept this life. I love books. Therefore I do not keep books.'

'But why? Why give up what you love?'

'One can't give up some things and keep others. To reject the materialism of this life one must reject even the pleasures of the intellect. Otherwise, accept it fully—as I did once—and savour the delights of the senses to the full. Don't do things by half-measures. I never believed in the middle way, in moderation in all things. It never satisfied me. I took every pleasure there was to take, and then, satiated, I took my leave of the world and all that it meant to me.'

'With no regrets?'

'With every regret.'

'Then, I ask again—why?'

'I can give you a hundred answers to your question, and all of them would be right, and yet none of them would be right. For there is not one answer, but many.'

He rises to stretch himself. He does so with a single elastic movement, without the help of his hands. There is hardly any flesh between his skin and his bones, but his skin is as tough as buffalo-hide. He must be impervious to wind and weather.

He looks out over the bare rolling hills and the valley and at the silver river twisting across the distant plain like some mythological serpent. It is the great river we see, most sacred of rivers. To bathe in its waters is to wash away all sin.

'Have you come from Kapila?'

'I am on my way there.'

Kapila lies on the banks of the river where it emerges from a gorge in the mountains. It is an ancient city, much favoured by the sages of old.

'The stones by the river are beautifully smooth,' he says. 'Once, picking one up I took it between my hot hands, polishing it with care. I did not find it round enough, and I threw it far into the river so that the water might rub away its angles for a few thousand years longer. To me, as to a stone, a thousand years are but a day.'

He sinks to his haunches again and his long hair falls across his shoulders hiding his face from me. Although he has rejected the past, he cannot help brooding upon it. We cannot destroy our memories until we have succeeded in destroying ourselves.

'Are you comfortable?' he asks.

'Not very, but I did not expect to find comfort here.'

'There are some old rugs and skins inside.'

'I am all right. It is cool out here.'

'The nights are cold. You will sleep in the cave with me?'

'I should be on my way.'

'You cannot reach Kapila tonight. There is no shelter between this place and the river.'

I do not say anything. I have a feeling that the cave will not welcome me. It has about it an aura of damp and decay, the sweetness of a corpse soaked in scented water. But at the same time I feel that if this recluse really wants me to stay, I will find it difficult to resist his will. Those who live alone can be very strong. Having mastered their own minds (or gone mad in the attempt), they have little difficulty in mastering the minds of others.

I see the pine-tops dipping gently on the next mountain, and a little later I feel the evening breeze on my cheeks. I am still young, and a cool uplifting breeze always stirs me to the marrow. It is the best aphrodisiac in the world.

○○○

THREE

∂Ω⊗

'The body of a woman,' he says, as though something of what I have been musing on has reached him, 'the body of a woman is an inexhaustible source of wonder and delight.'

I look at him with unfeigned surprise.

'Oh, of course I have finished with all that,' he says. 'That is obvious, isn't it? But, looking at me, you might get the impression that I have always been celibate. Nothing could be further from the truth. As a youth, I had an insatiable appetite for pleasure. It overrode all other considerations, I moved from one conquest to another in the single-minded pursuit of sexual pleasure. I suppose it was partly due to the woman servant who looked after me as a boy. She had some crazy idea that I was gifted with supernatural powers in these matters. She gave me strange potions and concoctions to drink!

'She was a big woman with broad hips and fleshy buttocks that quivered at every stride. Early every morning, even before the sun was up, she took me down the steps to bathe in the cold waters of the river. There was hardly anyone about at that time. Her huge, heavy breasts smelling of musk brushed against my cheeks as she poured the powerful waters over my head. She held me firmly between her thighs and laved my back with her rough hands. Later, in the small courtyard of our house, she would massage my limbs with mustard oil and with her fingers she would press at the root of my penis, a sensation both painful and pleasurable.

'Sometimes, when my parents were away, she would make me lie down with her, lie down upon her naked and mountainous flesh, and she would take my mouth between her heavy lips and thrust her tongue against mine. This kissing was always pleasurable and I never tired of it. I was a merry monkey, full of good intentions, trying to satisfy an elephant!'

'Stop!' I say, unable to control my laughter. 'Why do you tell me all this?'

'I thought you wanted to hear my story.'

'Did I say so? Well, I didn't think you would be so explicit.'

'Would you like a more romantic tale?'

'No. Carry on. Just so you finish it quickly and let me go my way.'

'Would you hear more of this woman who instructed me in the hidden arts of pleasure?'

'If she is relevant ...'

'Oh, but she is relevant. She was the sorceress who helped me become, not a god, but a satyr! There has been no romance in my life, no "falling in love" as you call it—except, perhaps, once, oh yes, once! From the beginning I was trained in the art of seduction, in the art of extracting from a woman all that she had to give—exhausting her, drawing on her hidden resources, feeding on her like a vampire, until she had nothing to give and was completely destroyed. Of course I did not reach this stage at that early age; but already at puberty, I was working towards it, I felt certain powers growing within me. It was power that I sought, not simply the appeasement of lust.

'A man who lived beside the river taught me to concentrate, to channelise my thoughts in such a way that I could gain a measure of mastery over the minds of others ... every day, for an hour, I sat cross-legged on a smooth earthen floor and gazed steadily at a small black phallus placed a few feet away from me. As I gazed upon the stone, it seemed to grow before me, swelling and throbbing, and I experienced the sensation of having discarded my own sack of a body to enter the substance of the stone. It was only momentary. A spider crawling over my foot brought me back to the reality of my material self. Many hours of concentration were to pass before I could ignore the movements of spiders or insects.

'At home I practised before a mirror, concentrating on the space between my eyebrows. This was strenous at first, and a throbbing headache would often result. But after a few weeks I found I could stand before the glass for an indefinite period, concentrating on the space between my eyes.

'I concentrated on sounds. I could close my eyes, admit into my mind one sound—the tinkling of a bell, or the dip of a tap—and live with that sound, to the exclusion of all else. After some time, the tinkle would become the clanging of many great bells or the drip of the tap would be a thunderous waterfall. I had to be shaken out of trances I had entered. My mother was worried about my strange behaviour. My father, whose many business interests absorbed his own sexual drive, could not be bothered. Only the woman servant, my mentor and aide, was pleased. Who was she and where did she come from? Nobody seemed to know. She had come to our house soon after I was born and had made herself so useful that my parents kept her even after I was long past my childhood. She had no children of her own but it was said that she had been married once, that her husband had died and left her very rich, and that she had squandered her money on some obscure cult. The more orthodox did not recognize this cult and associated it with sorcery.

'Well, it was sorcery of a kind.'

'Slowly I was developing my adolescent will to a point where I could impose it on others. I found it easier to do this when I closed my eyes. Then I could shut out all visual distractions and direct my thoughts towards the person I wished to influence. The first time I succeeded in doing this

I thought it was purely accidental. Perhaps it was, that first time; but its success gave me confidence in my growing powers.

'It was a warm, languid afternoon and I felt the slow turning of desire as I lay on the string cot in the bedroom. Through the half-open door I could see our servant stretched out on her cot, her waist bare, her hair loose, her lips slightly parted, her eyes only half-closed. (Even when she was sound asleep, her eyes were never completely closed.) Desire welled up within me. I longed for her harsh kisses and rough caresses. But nothing was possible with my mother present, and I found myself wishing that I could be so gifted with magic powers that I would be able to make people disappear (or appear) at will! This, I knew, could only be achieved after hundreds of years of training, and one had first to learn to live a hundred years! Our thoughts are so tame and timid to begin with that we seldom realize, until it is too late, what concentrated powers lie untapped in our minds. And for those who learn too quickly, there is madness ...

'But I turned towards my mother, and closing my eyes, directed my thoughts at her, willing her to leave the room, the house—go anywhere, do anything, until I willed her back again. For five minutes I assaulted her in this way, and when I opened my eyes I found her staring at me with a rather bewildered expression.

"What time is it?" I asked.

'She glanced at the small gold watch on her wrist and said, "It is only three ... Is there anything you want?"

' "No, but you asked me to remind you to go out at three o'clock." She had not made such a request but did not seem surprised at the suggestion. She got up slowly, stretched herself and went to the mirror to arrange her hair.

' "I have to go out at three," she said. "But I forget what I wanted ..."

' "You were to visit someone."

' "Yes, that's it. Thank you for reminding me. It's your

cousin Samyukta's birthday. Would you like to accompany me? They are always asking about you."

'No. I do not like them. Besides, I have a headache.'

' "Then I will wake Mulia and tell her to press your forehead."

' "It's all right, Mother. I will wake her myself when you have gone. Let her sleep a little longer."

'Mulia had been awake for some time and she came to me as soon as my mother left the house and began pressing my forehead, rubbing her thumbs over my eyelids and then pressing gently down on my temples. I let her do this for some time. I did have a headache, due perhaps to the effort I had made in shifting my mother from the house! It soon went, however, thanks to Mulia's ministrations.

'The voluptuous creature soon stood before me in all her monstrous beauty, a feast for the eye, a mountain worthy of conquest. I have never understood the misguided attitude of most people to heavy, fleshy women, who are generally considered ugly. Surely, in the generous abundance of their flesh, their broad dips and curves and gradual inclines—bodies where the questing lover may wander freely and unhindered; where he can stop and rest, or turn a corner and discover some hidden recess—surely these magnificient women have a marked superiority over those of a more conventional build? They have so much more to offer!

'Why go into detail? The memory no longer excites me and would only disturb your own peace of mind. I'm only trying to give you some idea of my development as a destructive force. Suffice it to say that my former governess was as thrilled as I at the achievement, and now declared herself to be my devoted paramour.

'Nor was it simply a matter of having qualified as a lover. The physical conquest was only half the victory. It could not have been achieved so completely without my having gained some command over her personality. Mulia had of course always intended that I should be hers. In spite of her imposing proportions, the strength of her arm, and her delightful witchcraft, her instincts were truly feminine. She had sought to conquer me only in order that she might be conquered. I had yet to impose my will on someone who resisted it. I had yet to enslave someone who held me in hatred and contempt. That would be the real challenge—the conquest, the ego-destruction of someone who had so far remained inviolate!'

ଞୠ

FOUR

ည္ဟ

'I must go now,' I say. 'It is not yet dark. I can be at the river before ten o'clock.'

'I advise you to stay,' urges my 'host'. 'It is not safe to walk these hills at night.'

'I am not afraid of wild animals.'

'Nor should you be, by day. But at night who is to tell which is beast and which is demon? For the evil spirits of these mountains, chained to the rocks by day, move abroad at night.'

'Do they trouble you, then?'

'They do not trouble me. I am too powerful for any kind of spirit save one—the spirit of an innocent! But come inside, it is getting cold out here.'

'It is dark in the cave.'

'I have a lamp. You have nothing to fear if you are pure at heart. Have you ever destroyed the soul of another human?'

'No.'

'Then what have you to fear?'

'Those who destroy souls.'

'Ah! Then you need not fear me, because I destroyed my last soul, my own, a long time ago.'

It is cold but dry inside the cave, which extends for some twenty feet into the side of the mountain. I sit down on a goat-skin and watch the recluse making a fire at the entrance to the cave.

'I will prepare some food for you,' he says.

'No, don't bother. I am not hungry.'

'As you wish. But I will light the fire to keep the animals

away. Sometimes I am visited by a leopard or a hyena.'

The fire throws a warm red glow over his emaciated frame, and for a moment or two, as his shadow leaps across the walls of the cave, he seems a little larger than life. When he turns to me, his body comes between me and the fire, and he is now a crouching black phantom, featureless, faceless, formless, who might at any moment leap upon me in the dark to suck the blood from my fingers and feet. But his voice, as always, reassures me.

'Do you mind if I talk?' he asks.

'Not at all. I have no desire to sleep.'

'Nor have I. When I sleep, I am defenceless. Then my mind is invaded by sirens and beautiful women with twisted feet, and young maidens covered with boils, and they ravish me and I am helpless against them. By day, I am master of my own mind, and remembered flesh cannot touch me.'

'So you have not entirely escaped the world you left behind?'

'It is another world that invades my soul. Sometimes I sit up into the early hours of the morning, so that I may avoid these visitations. For when they possess me, they drain me of all my strength, as I once drained others of their life-blood. But I will not trouble you with a tale of torment. I will tell you instead, of the powers I developed as a youth, and what use I put them to! Did I mention my cousin Samyukta?

'I did not like her and she did not like me. We bore each other hatred and malice—and that was enough to make us physically attractive to each other.

'She was a pretty girl, but coy and very aloof, and I resented her airs and graces. I was never much to look at, and whenever we were in the same room she behaved as though I did not exist, although she was perfectly aware of my presence. She did her best to humiliate me. If she said anything, it was to comment on the careless way in which I dressed. But I was indifferent to my appearance. People were not impressed with me until I spoke to them or until they came within the ambit of my questing mind. Once I was certain of my powers, I could dominate most individuals; but certain barriers had first to be broken down.

'Samyukta and I were of the same age, and at the time I am telling you about, we were seventeen or eighteen. Mulia now called me her young stallion. But cousin Samyukta, unaware of my gifts, treated me with contempt and laughed at me whenever we passed each other on the road.

'I had always looked away at her approach, and that had been my mistake. But my joustings with Mulia had given me a new confidence in the presence of women, and I knew that my cousin, for all her supercilious ways, was not very sure of herself. One day I saw her walking along the opposite pavement, accompanied by two girls, school friends. Before she could notice me, I crossed the road and was standing in her way. She gave a start, but before she could speak (and her words were to be avoided, for they were as poisoned·barbs), I fixed her eye with mine and held her motionless, while her expression changed from scorn to bewilderment to fear. At that moment, I am sure she felt I was capable of doing her violence. Later when we grew intimate, she swore that during that unexpected encounter she had seen a small yellow flame spring up in my right eye. I remember that she went pale, and when I saw her colour change I knew I had gained the ascendancy. I was so thoroughly aroused that I had difficulty in restraining myself from touching her on the street, in the presence of her friends. When I stood aside to let them pass, the colour flooded back to Samyukta's face, and she went strutting up the street, head in the air, as though she had just given me the snub of a lifetime.

'I smiled inwardly and walked home to Mulia. I told her of my intentions. She was not jealous. Knowing that she possessed my heart, she was prepared for others to possess my flesh.

' "But how do we arrange this?" I asked. "How do we get her here?"

' "We do not get her here. You go there, prince."

'But she has a mother and an aunt.'

' "They go out together on Saturday mornings. And on Saturday mornings Samyukta does not go to school. She prepares the midday meal, while her mother and aunt relax in the bazaar."

' "You are well informed, Mulia."

'She gave me a look of slavish devotion, took my hand and put my fingers to her lips. "You will never tire of me, will you?"

' "I will tire of you when you are old."

' "Ah! At least you do not try to deceive me."

' "You are not to be deceived."

' "No, but I am happy that you have told me the truth. I will preserve my burden of a body for another five, perhaps ten years, for as long as you desire it, and then I will go away."

'The next day Samyukta and her mother visited us. I did not make my presence felt, but sat quietly in a corner of the room, while tea was served. The woman talked about other women, the price of vegetables, and the horoscope of a certain young man who might be a suitable match for Samyukta. My cousin sat between her mother and mine, saying very little, but occasionally casting a glance in my direction. Outwardly, I paid no attention to her, but after some time I closed my eyes, and conjuring up a vision of her face, dwelt upon it for some time, turning my thoughts towards her, creating a flow of mental energy that I hoped would reach her in waves of telepathic power! My intention, of course, was to impose my will on her in such a way that she would be absolutely receptive when the right opportunity brought us together. I wanted to be sure of her response well in advance.'

'When I opened my eyes, I gazed full upon Samyukta. Her eyes were drawn inexorably to mine, and for more than minute we gazed intensely at each other, until even our mothers could not help noticing.

' "Why are you staring so?" asked Samyukta's mother, who was facing her daughter and had her back to me.

'And my mother, who could not see Samyukta's face said, "Do not stare like that, my son. You frighten me."

'My mother, a nervous creature, had in fact grown afraid of me during the past year or two. She could sense certain changes taking place in me without being able to understand them. She knew that Mulia and I were very close, and while she was relieved that I did not make too many demands on her, she was uneasy because I went to the servant woman with my confidences. Already dominated by my father, my mother was not one to assert herself in any way. She was content to put away money for my 'future' and to make occasional donations to the temples. She was certain that there was only one way into the hearts of the gods, and that was through the hands of the priests.

'And so, because my mother was frightened by my look, I turned my face to the window. A band of hermaphrodites was passing by in the street. Just then I longed to be one of them, the perfect synthesis of man and woman.

'Could Samyukta and I uniting lose our genders in each other and be as perfect as the hermaphrodites? For a few moments, perhaps; and then, uncoupled, we would lose ourselves again until guided by the itching of desire, we took refuge once more in each other's embrace.'

'When the confrontation did take plcae about a week later, it came as something of an anti-climax. She was no novice. There was no pearl to prise loose from its shell, no citadel to lay waste. Even so, it must have been a novel experience for her, because she did not expect an assault as fierce as mine. She swooned away before the hour was up. I waited until she opened her eyes, and then I assailed her again, until she moaned and scratched and bit. I had expected to stain her bed crimson with my lust. Instead it was she who drew blood. My arms and shoulders bore the wounds for weeks. Men have nothing to teach women. We can subdue women but we cannot teach them anything!

'Are you listening? Good. I am not trying to lecture you, nor do I wish to titillate you with an erotic tale. There is a principle contained in life that is more powerful than life itself. The body's rapture cannot be divorced from the rapture of the soul. It took me a long time to realize this. Certainly, at the age of eighteen, I had no thought for my soul. I believed in nothing, only love and its pleasures; and the strengthening of my mind and will was carried out with the object of gratifying my senses. I had no ambitions other than to glory in the delights that are there for all those who seek them—I was not interested in power or position. My father had money, and I was his only son. Therefore my first duty was to spend his fortune.

'My father, a man I hardly knew, had spent a lifetime in amassing wealth. He manufactured electric bulbs, shoe polish, and a hair-darkening cream. (The same ingredients went into both polish and cream.) On those rare occasions when he entertained his friends, he liked to tell them about the struggles of his youth and how he hawked his wares on the streets of Delhi. Although he had never been to school, he was determined that his son should receive the best possible education. After I had taken my degree, he would send me to Oxford!

'The thought of spending half my life in college horrified me. I was determined to fail my exams in order that I might discourage my parents from sending me to college. My father had lakhs of rupees, and competent managers to run his factories. I would be quite happy to take the money and leave the factories in the capable hands of his managers—they would see to it that the business continued to bring in profits. I could see no point in hoarding wealth and believed it to be a son's first duty to spend money as fast as his father could make it.

'My mother seemed to think so too, because though she was frugal by nature, she tried to get me the money I needed for my clothes, rings, watches, entertainments, and wines. She always gave me what I wanted, even if it meant dipping into her own allowance.

'My affair with cousin Samyukta was to last for over a year. But in the course of it I was to have several other adventures, some of them rather expensive. But I cannot dismiss Samyukta so quickly. She was a girl of some character, and when I look back on that wild and wilful time I realize that she had more to offer than most of the professional courtesans whom I visited from time to time. She did not give herself to me for mercenary reasons. I was a challenge to her own strong sensuous nature, and she matched my aggressive skills with her own passionate and fevered responses. She was one of those restless women whose physical demands can never be wholly satisfied. If I was with her, she was happy and satisfied; but if a few days passed and I could not visit her, she grew pensive, irritable, burning up in the fever of her own desire. We grew to like each other. That's strange, isn't it? Because we had never liked each other before.

'But of course there were a few other adventures.

'A youth of eighteen who suddenly finds himself a sexual warrior becomes quite rampant, and pursues his prey indiscriminately. Too indiscriminately for his own good. The pleasure houses of Kapila were few, and did not offer any very startling attractions. Most of the painted trollops were past their prime, and their patrons had first of all to be bemused with bhang or opium so that they did not look too closely at their battle-scarred partners.

'But there was one who was different ...'

&so;&og;

FIVE

80QB

'One evening, I pushed open the door of an old house teetering over the riverbank, and looked into a narrow passage dimly lighted by a green paper lantern. From within came the sounds of flute and sitar. A curtain was drawn back and an old woman came towards me. She was a withered old crone who glanced at me with an enticing leer and led me to the top of a staircase where she took my money with a swooping, gull-like movement. She then led me into a small, dark room where I was able to make out a wide couch, raised just above the floor and decorated with a gay but tattered rug.

' "I will fetch Shankhini for you,' she said. 'You will be happy with her."

'My eyes gradually grew accustomed to the dim light, and I was able to see the girl who entered the room and closed and bolted the door behind her. She drew near with a composed and friendly manner, as if I was an old acquaintance. And in some ways I suppose I must have been, for to the prostitute, all men are one—unity in diversity!

'Except for a diaphanous wrap of silk and a narrow girdle, the girl was completely naked. She wore white jasmine blossoms in her black hair. She looked little more than a child, although her hips were graceful and well-rounded.

' "Shall I dance?" she asked. "Tell me what you would like me to do.'

' "Dance," I said. I had been unprepared for her youthfulness.

'And so she danced beneath the greenish moon of the

paper lantern, and the only sound was the soft fall of her feet upon the mat. The heavy door shut out the music downstairs, the street-cries, the hollow boom of the river. It was a dance without music, without sound, and I felt as though those small feet were dancing gently on my heart, on the very source of my life. When the dancing ceased the girl smiled at me with an expression simultaneously wise, childlike, and passionate. Looking like a sleek green-gold cat in the light from the lantern, she subsided softly on to the couch beside me. She had been trained in the art of making love. And yet beneath it all lay an undercurrent of innocence. I think this was because she suffered from no feelings of guilt. She had been brought up to please men as though this was her sole duty in life. She had not known and did not seek any other kind of existence.

'She did not let a moment pass in which she did not seem to be giving herself. Her aspect was continually changing. She did not surrender even one of her secrets without giving me an inkling that another still remained to be disclosed.

' "Do you find me beautiful?" she asked. It was her stock question. And I gave her the expected answer: "You are the most beautiful girl I have ever seen."

'She smiled at me with her large, childlike eyes. Then her head came between me and the lantern, and her face seemed to be framed in a halo of green light.

' "Forget everything," she said. "Here there is no time, neither night nor day."

' "Let me do something for you," I said, feeling suddenly generous towards this girl. "Let me give you something."

' "I take nothing," she answered. "It is for the old woman to take. You must only tell me that I am beautiful and that I have made you happy."

' "You are very beautiful. You make me very happy."

' "I have heard it a hundred times. But I still like to hear it." And then, drawing close to me and gazing into my eyes

she said, "You are very important to yourself, are you not?"
She raised her hand to my brow, and tapping my temples
with her painted fingers, said: "There is a cold fire there! It is
stronger than all other flames, and seems brighter. It fights
against the warmth of the heart, and will quench the fire of
many hearts. So you must always move from one to another.
What are you looking for? There is nothing to find. Forget
everything. Love me, and forget!"

'Forget? Can the mind forget? It was written by a sage of old:
"Remember past deeds, O my mind, remember!" But the
injunction is unnecessary, because we are remembering all the
time—even when we say we have forgotten. And can the
memory of past deeds really shape the nature of future deeds?
Man cannot help but live in conformity with his nature; his
subconscious is more powerful than his conscious mind, and
he cannot deny his body until he removes himself from the
scene of all physical activity. It is useless to struggle against
one's nature. Some believe that there is salvation in struggle—
they are merely showing that they do not know what salvation
is.

'At first I sought to assuage my restlessness by communing
with nature. I searched for truth in the rippling of streams and
the rustling of leaves; in the blue heavens or the wilderness of
the jungle; in the behaviour of men, beasts and plants; in the
superabundance of sunshine that pours down in India. But
our bodies germinate as the resurrections of nature. Each
bubbling spring, swelling fruit or bursting blossom, reminded
me that I too was part of this burgeoning process, so that it
was not long before the throb in my loins was as tenderly
painful as the unfolding of a rosebud.

'I am not trying to give you the impression that those
years of youthful dissipation were interspersed with a vague

searching for my inner self. Once again, I have anticipated ... The search, if you can call it that, came later. I am merely trying to tell you how I came to be here. This cave is the end of all searching but before the search there was the indulgence, and the indulgence was a part of the process that brought me to this place.'

ॐ

SIX
ഇറ

'And meanwhile, I grew in Mulia's love.

'She tended me as a gardener tends a favourite plant, giving it all the water and nourishment it needs. Special sweets were made for me. Ancient recipes were turned up, and sherbets of many hues and flavours were given to me morning, noon and night. I had given up asking what they contained. I left everything to Mulia. She tried each portion before passing it to me, to make sure that the brew was not too potent. I was convinced that one day I would find her lying dead on the floor, poisoned by one of her own concoctions.

'But I was not the sort of person who could give anything in return for love. As soon as I found someone growing tender towards me, I withdrew into myself, became remote and cold, so that the love that might have been mine was squandered in an empty void. I was determined to leave them with a feeling of insufficiency. Those who gave themselves to me suffered for it. I became cruel and callous towards them. Was it victory I wanted, or the chance to spurn victory? Samyukta was made to suffer in this way. But Mulia, twenty years older than me, was an exception. I seldom withheld my affections from her, I knew that she was wholly for me and with me. My wealth, strength, welfare and happiness were her sole concern. I was the ruling passion of her life and I knew that if I was taken from her, she would lose the impetus for living.

'Shankhini, the woman who lived by night, was in a different category altogether. All men had immersed themselves in her, and she could not be expected to love an individual man any more than a man could be expected to love her. But what was the mysterious attraction that drew me back to her again and again? She had no hold over me. And the old crone who ran the house, certain that I was enamoured with the lithe and boyish figure of this unusual girl, put the price up at every visit. I did not care, I could afford it—or rather my father could afford it. It even gave me a sensuous thrill to hand over the money to the old woman. Not that the old woman excited me in any way; she would have found it hard to arouse a camel! But the business of handing over the money in exchange for an hour or two of personal possession, ownership, of the girl who lived always in green shadows, was a thrill in itself.

'But would I ever be able to arouse her to any degree of rapture? Although I restrained myself, and took the time and trouble to create in her some crisis of response, she seemed incapable of reaching a state of ecstasy and abandonment. There had been too many men, she told me. Coupling with them had become a mechanical process, and there was no intensity or pleasurable sensation in it. She went through the motions, expertly and in order to satisfy those who had paid for the pastime, but she could not be expected to enjoy the game herself.'

'So perhaps she was a challenge to me, and that was why I went to her. I wanted to elicit from her a genuine, not a trained response. I think she preferred me to most of her customers, many of whom were pot-bellied businessmen whose overburdened waistlines gave their manhood a shrivelled aspect. Obesity is not conducive to effective love-making.

'It may seem strange, but I liked to talk to Shankhini. In those days, there were few to whom I could talk freely. Mulia

was illiterate, and her talk was confined to practical affairs,
my needs and bodily functions. She had no other interest
outside her small world of service. My mother was old-
fashioned and superstitious and so we had very little to say to
each other. I hardly ever saw my father. Fellow students at
school and college considered me a snob, a wealthy aristocrat,
a privileged member of a feudal society. They envied me, and
were a little afraid of me too, because unlike others from
affluent families, I made no attempt to ingratiate myself with
them. Had I lavished money on a few young men, I would
soon have had a following, but I had no need of sycophants.
I could live with myself, and within myself, provided there
were always these women to bear the burden of my ego.

'Samyukta was intelligent, but there was no real meeting of
our minds—the relationship was purely sensual in nature. I
gave her the satisfaction she needed after she had exhausted
herself intellectually. She was studying medicine, and had to
work very hard. Whenever she stopped working, she wanted
to stop thinking. I could supply no intellectual need, nor was
that what she wanted. But when I moved within her, she cried
with ecstasy, she was convulsed with joy; but afterwards she
had little or nothing to say. She turned over, lay flat on her
belly, and slept.

'And so in the evenings, as the lights were lit in the bazaar,
and pilgrims placed little leaf-boats filled with rose petals on
the waters of the river, I made my way to the tall old house
with the green paper-lanterns, and asked for Shankhini.

'She was not always available in the evenings. So I took to
visiting her in the afternoons, when other men were busy
earning a living.

'The old woman told Shankhini I paid well, and so she
went out of her way to make me comfortable, to please me,
and to persuade me to come again. She did this as part of her
duty; but it wasn't all commercial enterprise. As familiarity
grew between us, we spent some time in talk. What did we

have to say to each other? I don't remember much of it, but this strange girl had evolved a philosophy of her own to deal with the situation she found herself in. It was all a question of doing one's duty, she said. Death was a duty, just as much as life was just another way of dying.'

∾⊹∽

SEVEN

ℰ∞ℛ

It has grown cold in the cave. While my ascetic host has been talking, using me as his confessor, the fire has died down. Outside, a jackal complains loudly, and the wind grows restless and rushes up and down the hillside, seeking entry into the cave. But we are well protected by rocks and overhang, and when this twentieth-century cave-dweller adds more sticks to the embers, the flames shoot up again, and the warmth reaches out to me and I reach out to the warmth, move closer, get up and stretch my limbs and then sit down again, while the man's eyes follow me with a bright, probing look.

'So far,' I say, 'so far, you have not told me anything very startling about yourself. You did nothing that would account for your giving up the pleasures you have described. I envy you some of your exploits, but they are not in themselves extraordinary. Many young men have visited prostitutes and have even found sensitive souls among them. And many young men have sought to go through their father's money. Some have sunk by stages into a hell of squalor and have been quite happy wallowing in their own filth. You did not sink very low. Your obsessions were not those of the pervert or psychopath. You were perhaps slightly more obsessed with sex than most, but apart from that your sex life appears to have been remarkably normal! Many young men would have done the same, given the opportunity.'

'I made my opportunities. I imposed my will on others. I cared for no one but myself.'

'I concede that.'

'And I am not even halfway through the story.'

'Ah, well, in that case ... I have no desire to sleep, and it isn't midnight yet. You were talking of Shankhini, the girl with the green-gold body.'

'Yes. She preserved a perfect body, almost as a challenge and a taunt to the shapeless creatures who came to her by day and by night. She gave them their money's worth like a true professional. She was well-versed in all the technicalities of love-making. She gave her customers her body but not her soul. She could not love men. Her love went to another, a dark girl from the coast who was also owned by the old woman. One day, entering the room unannounced, I found them in each other's arms, tenderly kissing each other. When they saw me standing there, they drew apart, unhurriedly and without any sense of guilt. Without a glance at me, the dark girl left the room.

' "You should not have come in without calling or knocking," said Shankhini.

' "There was no one about, and your door wasn't locked. Where's the old lady?"

' "She had to go out to collect some money. Sit down, and I will prepare some tea for you."

' "I stretched myself out on the couch and asked, 'Who was the girl with you?"

' "My friend. Why, did you like her? Would you like to go to her?"

' "I hardly saw her ..."

' "She is very beautiful. If you would like to go to her, I will tell the old one."

' "All right. If you don't mind, that is."

' "Why should I mind? It is my business to persuade you to keep coming here. If you tire of one of us, there is always another."

' "I haven't tired of you. I do not even know you as yet. But I thought you would mind because you seemed to like the girl."

' "I love her, but that does not interfere with our work. Men like you will come and go. Nalini and I will still be here."

' "Men like me ... Am I like other men?"

' "You want the same things, don't you?"

' "No. Most men only want to possess you physically. I want both your mind and your soul."

' "I do not have these things to offer you. I think, I feel, but I cannot share my thoughts and feelings with any man."

' "You can share them with Nalini?"

' "Here is the tea. Drink it, and tell me your pleasure."

'But after drinking the tea, I got up to go. "You are very irritable today," I said. "I will come again." She looked dismayed and urged me to stay. Perhaps she was afraid that I might not come again and that her mistress would be annoyed. The old woman was just outside the door.

' "He would like to see Nalini," said Shankhini.

' "No," I said. "Not today. Some other time."

'It was a frustrating day. Mulia was out shopping. Samyukta's house was full of people. It was as though, for a few hours, I had ceased to exist for them! Although I knew that they were completely unconscious of my restlessness, I harboured feelings of resentment towards them. I was being neglected! I suppose it's the lot of the only son to feel that way.

'I must have given you the impression that as a youth I was obsessed with sex to the exclusion of all else, and that I was devoid of finer feelings. It is true there was a time when I believed that although all men were born equal, some men turned out to be more virile than others!

'As for falling in love, I had no idea what it was about. Loving (I was told) is giving, but at the time I was interested only in taking.

'Have I given you the impression that my life was spent entirely in the company of women? I had not made friends at college, but then, I seldom attended college. I found the lectures boring and a waste of time. I had nothing against books and even read some poetry, but I did not want life second-hand, from books. Mine was not a reflective nature—not then, anyway—and I could not reconcile mental pursuits with the pursuit of physical delight. And what would be the use of a degree in the Arts if I was going to spend the rest of my life helping my father to manufacture electric bulbs?

'When my father asked me to go to Delhi on his behalf, to attend an industrial exhibition that was being held in the capital, I agreed to do so. It was my father's intention to get me involved in the business. I was not interested in industrial exhibitions but I felt like a change from my confined life in Kapila and I set out with a sense of impending adventure. I had no idea where the adventure, if it came, would lead me. My father had given me five hundred rupees, and I would follow my fancy in seeing where it would take me and what I could do with it.'

&?&

EIGHT

৪৩৫৫

'My train rushed into the darkness, the carriage wheels beating out a steady rhythm on the rails. The bright lights of Kapila were swallowed up in the night, and new lights—dim and flickering—came into existence as we passed small villages. A star falls, a person dies. I used to wonder why I did not see more shooting stars, because in India someone is dying every minute. And then I realized that with someone being born every half-minute, falling stars must be in short supply.

'The people in the carriage were settling down, finding places for themselves. There were about fifty of us in that compartment sharing the same breathing space, sharing each other's sweaty odours.

'At four in the morning I woke from a fitful sleep to find the train at a standstill. There was no noise or movement on the platform outside. It was a very small station, and the train for some mysterious reason of its own had stopped there longer than usual, so that those in the train who had woken up had gone to sleep again, and those few who had been spending the night on the platform slept on as though nothing had happened. This was not their train.

'I watched them from the window. A very small boy was curled up in a large basket. His mother had stretched herself out on the platform beside him. A coolie slept on a platform bench. The tea-stall was untenanted. A dim light from the assistant stationmaster's office revealed a pair of sandalled feet propped up against a mountain of files. A bedraggled crow perched on the board which gave the station its name:

Deoband. The crow cawed disconsolately, as if to imply that this dismal wayside station was none of its doing. And yet— Deoband!—the name struck a chord. Wasn't this, by tradition, the most ancient town in India?

'The engine hissed, sending waves of hot steam into the fresh early morning air. My shirt clung to me. We were all smelling of perspiration. There had been no rain for a month but the atmosphere was humid, there were clouds overhead, dark clouds burgeoning with moisture. Thunder blossomed in the air.

'The monsoon was going to break that day. I knew it, the birds knew it, the grass knew it. There was the smell of rain in the air. And the grass, the birds and I responded to this odour with the same sensuous longing. We would welcome the rain as a woman welcomes a lover's embrace, his kiss, the fierce, fresh thrust of his loins after a period of abstinence.

'Suddenly I felt the urge to get out of that stuffy, overcrowded compartment, away from the sweat and smoke and smells, away from the commonplaces of life, from the certainty of my destination and predestined future. I would be a free wanderer, the last in a world where even the poets had retreated into the sculleries of their minds.

'I knew where I was supposed to be going: Delhi. I knew what I was supposed to do there—take the fatal step towards respectability. To be respectable—what an adventure that would be! And this prospect of an ordered, organized life frightened me. I knew that I could not put it off forever, but perhaps it could be postponed. I had five hundred rupees in my vest pocket. It would provide me with freedom for two weeks, perhaps three if I was not too extravagant. Five hundred rupees; the smell of coming rain; and outside, an unknown town. The combination was too strong for my wayward spirit.

'I clambered over my fellow passengers, my suitcase striking heads, shoulders, backsides. Grunts and curses followed me to the door. And then the train began to move. I was seized with panic. If I didn't get off quickly, I would never get off. I would be frozen forever into a respectable bulb manufacturer!

'I flung the door open and tumbled on to the platform. My suitcase spun away, hit the corner of a bench, burst open. The crow flew off in alarm. A dog began barking.

'The train moved on to Delhi, carrying with it six hundred souls in bondage, while I stood alone on the platform, in temporary possession of my own soul.

'The suitcase, which never locked properly, was soon closed. I looked furtively around. The coolie was still asleep—obviously no one ever got off at Deoband at that hour—or he would have grabbed my insignificant burden, carried it for a distance of twenty feet, and charged me a rupee. I needed my rupees. I could no longer scatter them about at random or live on credit as I did in my home town.

'I walked quietly to the turnstile. There was no one there to ask me for my ticket. I walked out of the station and found myself in wasteland of nondescript shacks—some of them labourers' huts, some warehouses, one or two of them uninviting tea shops. The scene was a dismal one, and if the train had still been at the station I would have returned to it and gone to Delhi. But so far in my defiance of the gods, I had done quite well, and it would have been admitting defeat to have returned to the station to hang around waiting for another train.

'By evening I was still disconsolately on a small hotel balcony overlooking the street, telling myself that I was a fool. For three hours nothing had happened to me, and now it looked as though nothing was going to happen. There was no Mulia to press my aching limbs, no Samyukta to ravish, no Shankhini to battle with my ego. My only acquisition was a headache from drinking too much of the local beer and sleeping too long under the electric fan.

'The camel had gone from across the street, but in its place was a buffalo. The traffic had increased, there were more people in the street. There were also more flies on the balcony, and one of them came buzzing into my half-empty glass in an effort to drown itself in what remained of my drink. It was a suicidal kind of evening. I rescued the fly from my glass, placed it gently on the balcony railing and watched it crawl groggily away. But my compassion was wasted. As the fly neared the wall, a gecko, chuckling greedily, swooped on the insect and gobbled it up.

'There was no one to talk to. The hotel manager was a moron, and the bearer's thoughts dwelt on the contents of my suitcase. A large drop of water hit the balcony railing, darkening the thick dust on the woodwork. A faint breeze sprang up, and again I felt the moisture, closer and warmer.

'Then the rain approached like a dark curtain. I could see it marching down the street, heavy and remorseless. It drummed on the corrugated tin roof and swept across the road and over the balcony. I sat there without moving, letting the train wet my sticky shirt and gritty hair.

'Outside, the street rapidly emptied. The crowd dissolved in the rain. Stray cows continued to rummage in dustbins, buses and tongas ploughed through the suddenly rushing water. A group of small boys, now gloriously naked, came romping along the street which was like a river in spate. When they came to a gutter choked with rain water, they plunged in, shouting their delight to whoever cared to listen. A garland of marigolds, swept from the steps of a temple, came floating down the middle of the road.

'The rain stopped as suddenly as it had begun. The day was dying, and the breeze remained cool and moist. In the brief twilight that followed, I was a witness to the great yearly flight of insects into the cool brief freedom of the night.

'It was the hour of the geckos. They had their reward for weeks of patient waiting. Plying their sticky pink tongues, they devoured insects as swiftly and methodically as Americans devour popcorn. For hours they crammed their stomachs, knowing that such a feast would not be theirs again. Throughout the entire hot season the insect world prepared for this flight out of darkness into light, and not one survived its bid for freedom.'

'I had walked the streets of the town for over three hours, and it was past midnight. Shop fronts were shuttered, the cinema was silent and deserted. The people living on either side of the narrow street could hear my footsteps, and I could hear their casual remarks, music, a burst of laughter.

'A three-quarter moon was up, shining through drifting, breaking clouds, and the roofs and awnings of the bazaar, still wet, glistened in the moonlight. From a few open windows fingers of light reached out into the night. Who could still be up? A shopkeeper going through his accounts, a college student preparing for his exams, a prostitute extricating herself from the arms of a paramour who had suddenly fallen asleep ...

'Three stray dogs were romping in the middle of the road. It was their road now, and they abandoned themselves to a wild chase, almost knocking me down. A jackal slunk across the road, looking to right and left to make sure the dogs had gone. A field rat wriggled its way through a hole in a rotting plank, on its nightly foray among sacks of grain and pulses.

'As I passed along the deserted street under the shadow of the clock tower, I found a young man, or a boy (I couldn't tell which) sleeping in a small recess under a rickety wooden staircase. He was wearing nothing but a pair of torn, dirty shorts—his shirt, or what was left of it, had been rolled into a pillow. He was sleeping with his mouth open; his cheeks were hollow, and his body, which looked as though it had been strong and vigorous at one time, was emaciated.

'There was no corruption, no experience on his face. He looked quite vulnerable, although I suppose he had nothing much to lose in the material sense.

'I passed by, my head down, my thoughts elsewhere—that is how we of the towns and cities usually behave when we see a fellow human lying in the gutter.

'And then I stopped. It was almost as though the bright moonlight had stopped me. And I started myself with the question, "Why do I leave him there? And what am I doing here anyway?"

'I walked back to the shadows where the boy slept and looked at him again. He seemed a very heavy sleeper, the sort of person who can fall asleep anywhere, at any time, oblivious to all that goes on around him. I coughed loudly, but nothing happened; I whistled, but still he slept; I picked up an empty can and dropped it beside him, but the noise had no effect on the sleeper. In his dreams he was elsewhere, moving among the spirit-haunted mountains, while his material body lay in this town. I found myself wishing that I could sleep like that— it was the sleep of one who was protected by his own innocence.

'I went down on my knees and touched the boy's shoulder. But he must have been touched often in his sleep. His lips moved slightly, but there was no alteration in the rhythm of his breathing.

'One arm was thrown back, and I noticed a scar under his armpit where the hair began. Looking at that scar, all the warnings of Mulia and my mother crowded in upon me—tales of crime by night, of assault and robbery. But when I looked again at the untroubled face, I saw nothing there to disturb me.

'And since he did not wake, and seemed comfortable, why did I not stand up and walk away and take the morning train to Delhi? I still do not know. Something was pressing me on, urging me to shake the boy out of his slumber.

'I took him by the shoulders and gave him a good shaking. He woke with a loud cry, as from a nightmare, and stared at me with something like terror. He sat up, cringing away, holding his hands before his face. But then, when he realized that I was a man and not the demon of his dream, his fear turned to indignation.

' "Who are you? What do you want?"

' "Nothing," I said, standing up and moving away. ' "I did not see you there. I am sorry to wake you."

'I moved a few steps away, then stopped and looked back at the youth. He was still crouching on the steps, still staring at me, but he had lost both his fear and his anger, and he was only a little puzzled by this apparition in the middle of the night.

' "Haven't you anywhere to stay?"

'He shook his head.'

'Perhaps the tone of voice I used gave him some confidence, because the hostility left his face and in its place I saw a glimmer of hope.'

'I had committed myself. I could not pass on.'

' "Do you want a job?" I asked.

' "No."

' "You have money?"

' "No."

' "Do you want some money?"

' "No, babuji."

' "Then what do you want?"

' "I want to go home."

' "Where is your home?"

' "In the hills."

' "Far away?"

' "Yes, babuji. In the Jalan hills."

' "And how much does it cost to get there?"

' "Twenty rupees."

' "And how much have you got?"

‘ “One rupee.”

'He held his torn shirt in his hands. It was his only possession. I liked his open look, the way he returned mine without any attempt at evasion.

‘ “I'll see that you get home,” I said. “On one condition.”

'A shadow of doubt passed across his mobile face. (It was no mask, that face.)

‘ “Babuji—I have never done anything—anything shameful.”

‘ “Shameful? You have not heard my condition. What did you think I was going to ask you to do—sleep with me?”

'He laughed and looked embarrassed.

'I said, “Don't be an ass. I have always taken my pleasure with women. Listen to my condition before you start getting nervous.”

'He did not say anything but kept twisting his shirt in his hands—he was no longer looking me in the eye.

‘ “I was about to say that I'd help you to get home provided you took me with you. I would like to see your hills.”

'His dark, sombre face lit up. He smiled like an angel. All the latent hospitality of his tribe welled up and burst through the barrier of his poverty.

‘ “Oh, I will take you to my home, babuji. I have nothing here, but in the hills I have a house, fields, a buffalo! Yes! I will take you to my home.”

'No longer hesitating, he came to me, brimming over with a simple trust and joy. I could not betray that trust, nor could I fail to trust him. I was committed to a stranger in the night. I had sought him out deliberately, imposed my will on him, and the consequences of the meeting would be entirely of my own making.

'And so there were two of us on that lonely street. The rain had held off just long enough for the encounter. Soon it began to drizzle.

‘ “We will go to my hotel,” I said. “Have you anything to

bring with you?"

' "Nothing," he said. "Yesterday I sold my shoes."

' "Never mind. Let us get some sleep while the night remains with us. Tomorrow, in the morning, we will leave this place. It has served its purpose, and now there is nothing to keep me here. Nothing to bring me back again."

'The boy lay on the mattress which I had removed from the bed and placed on the floor. His face was in darkness but the light from the veranda bulb fell across his legs. There was no escape from my father's bulbs! I lay flat on my belly on the string cot, while the ceiling-fan hummed in the moist air immediately above me.

' "Are you awake?" I called.

' "Yes," said the boy.

' "The mosquitoes make it difficult to sleep. So let us talk. Tell me, how do we get to your village?"

' "It is a difficult place to reach," he said.

' "Well, if it was easy to reach, there would be no point in my going there. Will we have to walk a lot? I have not done much walking."

' "We must walk about thirty miles. But first we must take a train or a bus. Later we walk."

' "Good. And now tell me your name."

' "Roop."

' "You have brothers and sisters?"

' "A brother, no sisters. My brother is younger than me and goes to school. I never went to school. There was another brother, but he died—he was attacked by a leopard, and the wounds were so bad that he died after several days."

'After a brief silence, he asked, "Why do you wish to visit my home, babuji?"

' "Because it is far away. Because I am bored with my own home. I have a mother and father and servants, but I am bored with all of them."

'Roop was one of those people blessed with the gift of

being able to sleep sweetly and soundly through cannon-fire and earthquake. Once he fell asleep, there was little that could wake him. The morning sun embraced him, moved lovingly over his dark gleaming body, touched his eyelids, settled on his untidy hair. Still he did not wake. He slept on as though drugged. I called him, I shouted, I reached out and shook him by the shoulder, but he did not stir. A fly settled on his lips, but although his mouth twitched, he did not open his eyes.

' "One of us will have to get up," I muttered, looking at my expensive smuggled watch which showed nine o'clock. "Otherwise we won't get anywhere today."

'And I wanted to get away as soon as possible. The urge to stop at Deoband had been strong, but the urge to move on was stronger. During the night I had dreamt of pine forests and mountain streams, pale pink flowers growing in the clefts of rocks and fair hill maidens bathing beneath pellucid waterfalls.

'I got up and sprinkled water on Roop's face. Nothing happened. I placed my foot on his broad heavy thigh and shook him vigorously. But he simply smiled. He was still dreaming—of a girl, perhaps; or possibly of the chicken we had eaten on returning to the hotel the previous night.

'I decided that I would have to use some more positive method of rousing Roop. Shaking him was of no use, slapping his face would have been impolite. So I compromised—held the water-jug over his head and kept pouring until he awoke, spluttering and shaking his head and greeting the day (and me) with foul language.

'An hour later—my purse considerably lightened by our short stay at the hotel—we were sitting in a bus and moving hopefully in the direction of the hills.'

৪০০৪

NINE

෨෬

'It had been raining all morning, and whenever there were dips in the road, the bus sent up sprays of muddy water. Sometimes the rain came in at the windows and wet my shirt. But I did not close the window, it was too stuffy in the bus, and the reek of cigarettes and beedis added to my discomfort.

'Let us be grateful for neem trees. Their pods had fallen on the roadside, and these, bursting or being crushed against the wet earth by passing vehicles, emitted a powerful but pleasant odour which drifted in through the window on the breeze.

'The road was straight, but the bus was continually having to swerve or brake to avoid coming into collision with the slow and ponderous bullock-carts that came lumbering and creaking down the middle of the highway. In the fields, the ploughing had begun. Long wooden ploughs yoked between two bullocks raked crooked furrows in the softened earth. A heron stood on one leg in a rice field. An egret perched behind a buffalo's ear, searching there for tender insects.

'The buffaloes were of course in their element. With tanks and ditches overflowing, they did not have to search for muddy water in which to wallow through the long hot days. Some were already knee-deep among the water-lilies. Their dung, as always, was precious, and I remember the quaint spectacle of a farmer, realizing that one of his buffaloes was about to give forth riches, taking up his position behind the heaving beast and collecting a generous amount of dung in his arms, even as it fell. Hot and fresh it must have been! A second later, and this precious product would have been lost forever in the lily-pond.

'Yes, I remember that bus ride. Who remembers bus journeys? They are always so monotonous. But I remember that one, because it was a monsoon day and I was moving towards the unknown.

'The bus moved past a score of naked children romping in the rain; past a tonga-load of villagers, drenched but merry; past a young man with a dancing bear; past a sugar factory; past a railway crossing, mercifully open; past a dead cow, dense with vultures; past tiny huts and huge factory buildings.'

'I woke to what sounded like the din of a factory buzzer but was in fact the voice of a single cicada emerging from the lime tree near my bed. A faint light was breaking over the mountains. The morning air was quite chill, and I moved closer to Roop for warmth. We had slept out of doors, sharing the same bed.

'His mother and young brother, who slept indoors, had thought me a little strange for wanting to sleep outside. Most hill people prefer to sleep inside the small stuffy rooms of their rough stone houses, even when the nights are warm. It has something to do with their fear of the dark, their belief in demons and malignant spirits who dwell in trees or take possession of the bodies of leopards and sometimes humans. Roop told me that he had seen the ghost of a woman who had been at least ten feet tall, and whose feet faced backwards. His strong belief in demonlore made him reluctant to join me outside; at the same time, he did not want to have his guest spirited off in the night. It would have been impolite on his part to leave me to the tree-spirits. His natural sense of hospitality overcame his naturally superstitious nature, and he joined me on the cot in the bright moonlight. No electric bulbs in his village—I had escaped my father at last!

'Once Roop was asleep, he was immune to all the spirits of the dead, being even more comatose than a corpse. The shrieking cicada had no effect on him. He slept with abandon, one leg thrown over my thigh, an arm hanging down from the side of the bed, his head thrown back, his mouth open in disregard of his own warning that spirits enter people through the mouth.

'As the sky grew lighter, I could see through the pattern of glossy lime-leaves the outlines of the mountains as they strode away into an immensity of sky. I could see the small house, standing in the middle of its narrow terraced fields. I could see the other houses, standing a little apart from each other in their own bits of land.

'I could see trees and bushes, and a path leading up the hill to the deodar forest on the summit. A couple of fruit trees grew behind the house.

'The tops of the distant mountains suddenly lit up as the sun torched the snow peaks. A door banged open. The house was stirring. A cock belatedly welcomed the daylight and elsewhere in the village dogs were barking. A magpie flew with a whirring sound as it crossed the courtyard and then glided downhill. Everyone, everything—except Roop beside me—came to life.'

'I was conscious of being observed. There was no one behind me, no one at the foot of the bed. But there was a soft footfall close by. I closed my eyes, pretended I was asleep. When I opened them, I found myself gazing into light brown eyes flecked with green—the fair complexioned face of Roop's younger brother. He had been looking at me with considerable curiosity because the night before, when I arrived, it had been dark and he had not been able to see me properly.

'When I returned his gaze, he smiled. He did not resemble Roop Singh at all, except in the sturdiness of his physique. He looked sensitive, reserved. The smile was shy, self-protective.

' "Is it time for us to get up?"

'He shook his head. "No, you can sleep. I have to go to school."

' "Your school starts very early."

' "It is very far," he said. "Five miles." And then, anxious to avoid further questioning, he ran off.

'The sun was up. It slipped across the courtyard and into the newly ploughed field and ran over the tips of the young maize that had come up with the first rain. It was time to get up.

'Roop's mother was a strong, handsome widow of about thirty-five. Those with conventional notions of beauty would not have called her good-looking. Some would have thought her ugly. Huge silver earrings passed through the tops of her ears, turning them inwards, elongating them, twisting them out of their natural shape. Those huge, imprisoned ears were inclined to divert one's attention from the rest of her face. The forehead was narrow, but the eyes were large and attractive. The nose was a strong one, having withstood the weight of another large silver ring. She wore a silver bracelet and silver bangles clashed at her ankles. All her savings had gone into silver ornaments. It wasn't safe to wear or keep gold.

'Her voice was deep and resonant without actually being masculine in tone. She had strong hands, large heavy feet—she walked barefoot even on the rocky hillsides.

'Roop was rather afraid of her. The younger brother loved her deeply.

'She gave us a heavy breakfast of curds and black mandwa bread and hot sweet tea.

'She did not look directly at me, but all the time I felt that she was watching me.'

❧∞❧

TEN

ಬಿಣ

'I was to be enslaved by this woman in a way that no woman had ever been enslaved by me. As the days passed, I became aware of her strange and powerful matriarchal passion. It was not the passive worship of Mulia, but something quite different.

'Strangely enough, I had not at first thought of her in terms of passion. Her physique did not attract me. True, Mulia was strong too, but that was because she was heavy, a mountain of flesh; otherwise she was a soft, feminine creature. But there was no surplus flesh on this woman of the mountains. She was hard, even muscular. Her feet were longer and much broader than mine. Her legs, which I glimpsed whenever she climbed the steep path to the fields, were the legs of an athlete. She had strong arms and lifted sacks of grass or bags of grain with an ease and facility that would have been the envy of most men.

'There was nothing delicate or pretty about her, but her face was strong and handsome, and her eyes, although lacking tenderness, were expressive and of dark spiritual intensity. She laboured more like a pack-mule than a man, but there were powerful, unquenched fires smouldering within her.

'Three days passed before she spoke to me, and then it was to ask me if I felt tired. Roop and I had returned after a long walk to a famous waterfall. We came back very hungry and with our limbs aching from the effort of climbing up two steep valleys. His mother prepared tea for us and when she handed my glass to me, she looked straight into my eyes and asked, "Are you tired?"

' "Yes," I said. "Very tired."

' "Tomorrow you will rest."

It rained heavily that night and all next morning.

'Only at noon did the clouds begin to break up and then the sun came through, gleaming gold on the green slopes. I remember a flock of parrots swooping low over the house, their wings flashing red and gold and blue. They settled in the oak trees. Roop Singh had gone to the next village, where there was a shop, to buy salt and soap.

'I walked through the fields till I came to a grassy slope. Then the sun seduced me, and I took off my clothes and lay stretched out on the grass. I fell asleep—for how long, I could not tell—but when I woke, I felt curiously relaxed, languid, even light-headed. I passed my hand over my forehead and felt something sticky; then, looking at my hand, I found it was covered with bright red blood.

'I sat up, and got the fright of my life. My entire body was covered with leeches.

'They had crawled on to me while I was sleeping, had fastened on to my succulent flesh—as you must know, the bite of the leech can hardly be felt—and had then proceeded to gorge themselves on my blood. I now had about thirty leeches on my face, arms, chest, belly, backside and legs. One or two had had their fill and fallen off, leaving tiny punctures from which the blood trickled freely. One particularly fat leech—it was about two inches long—was feeding near my navel. I tried to pull it away, but it was stuck fast.

'I remembered being told that it was a mistake to remove leeches by force. The bite sometimes became septic. They would fall away and dissolve if a little salt was applied.

'I sprang to my feet, gathered up my clothes, and ran naked through the ploughed field until I reached the house. Seeing no one about I rushed indoors, surprising Roop's mother who was lighting a fire.

'If she was surprised at my condition, she did not show it.

' "Look, mother of Roop," I said, addressing her directly

for the first time. "I'm covered with leeches. Give me salt."

'She got up from the fire, came nearer to examine me (it was always dark indoors) and said, "There are too many. Come into the other room, I will remove them for you."

'Armed with a container of salt, she led me into the next room and then started applying salt to the leeches. One by one, they squirmed and twisted and fell off.

'As they fell, they burst open and my blood oozed out of their slowly dissolving bodies, staining the floor. Little rivulets of blood kept trickling down from the open wounds on my body, which took a long time to close up.

' "I must have a bath," I said.

' "No. Let the blood dry on you. Only then will the bleeding stop."

'So I sat down on the floor feeling rather foolish, while Roop's mother watched me gravely from their doorway. If only she'd smiled or laughed, I would not have felt so uneasy. But she watched me intently, her seemingly dispassionate gaze taking everything in.

'It was an unusual situation for me. I had been in the habit of gazing upon the attributes of women. Now the positions were reversed, and a woman, fully clad, was studying my anatomy. I felt defenceless, rather as though I was a male spider or scorpion about to be first mated and then devoured by the female.'

'She came to me that night. I had been feeling the humidity and slept on the veranda, while Roop, afraid of the early morning chill, slept indoors with his brother.

'I woke from a sound sleep to find someone lying beside me. Automatically, and from force to habit, I moved to one side. I stretched out an arm and my hand encountered those heavy earrings and twisted ears. Hastily, I drew my hand away; but I could not leave the bed. The woman's strong arms were around me, her powerful legs held me in a vice. Her breath, smelling of cloves, almost overpowered me.

'She did not attempt to kiss me. Kissing was obviously something foreign to her nature. But she began to stroke me with her large, rough hands; and aroused, I could not help but respond.

'This was a reversal of the usual role. She was active rather than passive in her attitude.

'Her breasts were huge pendulous things. Her arms and legs were much stronger than mine. Always proud of my virility, I now felt as though I would be inadequate for this woman who did not flinch, but who took me in her powerful arms and pressed upon me until I gasped for breath and wanted to cry for help.

'She did not give me any rest. She worked on me with her hands until I was roused again, and then she mastered me with complacent efficiency. Nothing seemed to happen to her. She could not be satisfied. She was some kind of vampire, a succubus—I swear to it—and she was determined to drain me of my last ounce of manhood.

'Only towards morning, when first light showed in the sky, did she leave me, returning to her own room. I lay limp and exhausted. I had done nothing to quench her passion and I knew that she could overpower me again at the first opportunity.'

ഇൽ

ELEVEN

ಬಿಇಜ

During our long vigil in the cave, the fire has gradually
died down. It is about four in the morning, and a faint light
appears on the snow of the Bandarpoonch massif. I am feeling
cold; but with sunrise only two hours away, I am able to
summon enough patience and fortitude to bear the gnawing
discomfort that has crept over me.

'Well—and then what did you do?' I ask.

'I ran away. Oh, not immediately. That would not have
been possible. She watched over me wherever I went. She
fattened me up with chicken and gave me strange sherbets to
revive my flagging virility. It was Mulia all over again, but I
was not the man who had tamed Mulia. I was in the hands of
a lioness, a woman far stronger, both mentally and physically,
then Mulia had ever been. Whereas once I had imposed my
will on others, I now found myself squirming under another's
will. Roop's mother fed me on reviving herbs and fluids only
in order that she might drain me of my strength. She was a
rakshasni prepared to reduce me to skin and bone, to suck me
dry!'

'And what of Roop—did he know what was happening?'

'He was too simple to comprehend. And he was too busy
wenching with the village girls. He was a randy fellow, poor
Roop. But the younger brother, he knew ... He would wake
up in the night, and tossing about restlessly, he would hope
to disturb us, to put an end to the ravishing of my body. But
she was in no mood to be bothered by minor distractions.

'And yet, there was a tremendous innocence about the way
in which this single-minded woman had stripped me of my

manhood and pretensions. Hers was the overpowering innocence of the mountains—I was helpless before it, just a computer lover overpowered by natural forces. She was not a scheming woman. She sought to appease a basic hunger, and she did so without a civilized veneer, without the cover of sophisticated talk. We who have grown up in the cities cannot understand the innocence of mountain people, because we cannot understand the innocence of mountains, high places which have retained their power over the minds of men because they still remain aloof from the human presence, barely touched by human greed. In the cities it is easy to despise those who live in awe of the mountains, because in the cities there are vehicles and noise and lights to hold at bay that fear of the dark which is the beginning of religion; but on the far hills the darkness is still terrible.

'And mountain people still keep some of their primal innocence. It can be disconcerting to one who is accustomed to the corruption of the cities, but unaccustomed to the simple terror and solitude of the hills, I was used to being the ravisher. I was now being ravished.'

'Had another man violated me, I would not have found it as humiliating as the experience of being violated by this unlettered woman with the heavy feet and long twisted ears. It was not only my manhood that she stripped; it was my beloved ego.

'Roop's younger brother helped me get away. He had been in sympathy with me from the first, had sensed my predicament, my helplessness.

'Roop's mother had the custody of my suitcase which was locked in the storeroom. Having no need of any money in the village—there was nothing to spend it on—I had kept my remaining cash, about three hundred rupees, in the suitcase. I knew I wouldn't get very far without any money, and I was equally certain that Roop's mother would not give it to me— she had no intention of letting me get away.

'When the boy asked me, "Will you walk with me to my

school?", I almost said no. The pleasures of walking did not appeal to me just then. But something in his expression told me that his intentions went deeper than what his words implied. He was not asking me to accompany him, he was urging me to do so.

'Puzzled, I said I'd come. His mother did not try to restrain me—she was confident that I would be back.

'We took the path to the stream, then followed the watercourse for a mile or two until that path forked, one branch twisting up the mountain on our right, the other keeping to the stream and running straight up the valley.

' "I will leave you here," said the boy.

' "Don't you want me to come as far as the school?"

He shook his head. "No. You should go now." He opened the satchel which contained his school books, and took out my wallet. "The money is all there," he said.

'I took the wallet and thanked him; then I offered him a hundred-rupee note.

' "That is not why I brought it," he said.

'He smiled and started climbing the steeper path. Where the path went round the hillside he turned and waved to me. Then he disappeared round the bend and went out of my life—my first and only friend.'

∞∞∞

TWELVE

ဢ೦೧

'Soon it began to rain. But I did not seek shelter. I walked ten miles in pouring rain until I reached the bus terminus. I was very tired when I got there and was tempted to spend the night in one of those seedy little hotels that spring up like mushrooms near every bus-stand; but I was afraid that Roop may have been sent after me, to try and persuade me to return. I caught the last bus to the plains, and the following day I was back in Kapila, secure among the anonymous thousands who throng the waterfront.

'My parents did not ask me too many questions. They were glad enough to see me back. At least, my mother was glad. She did not have long to live and I think she knew it. She had suckled and spoilt me and wanted to see me happy. My father would probably not have minded if I had disappeared for ever. He hadn't much confidence in me, and knew I would never be of any help to him in the business. I've no doubt he was furious with me for having wandered off on my own instead of going to Delhi, but to humour my mother, he said nothing. She thought I'd run away from home. Now that I was back, she was ready to indulge my every whim. Instead of getting less money, I was given more. And if I did not attend college, no questions were asked. No prodigal son ever had it better. And in this way young men are ruined for life.

'Although my mother adored me, under the delusion that I was a favourite of the gods, Mulia fussed over me more like a mother—or rather, like a brooding hen. Who would have thought that I was almost twenty ...

'Strangely enough, I found that I had grown indifferent to

Mulia. Had she changed, or had I? Had she grown older, flabbier, heavier, uglier—or was it that I now looked only for the ugliness instead of for the beauty? The strong odour of her body, which formerly had aroused me so easily, now failed to excite me. Instead I found myself disliking the odour. Strange, isn't it, how things that attract us become, after a period of time, the things that repel us ...

'I spoke to Mulia as before, but I avoided being alone with her. If my mother went out, I found some excuse for going out too. Mulia was constantly seeking opportunities for being alone with me; I was ever alert, ready to slip away.

'Still, the confrontration had to come.

'I slept late one morning and did not know that my mother had gone out early. The air of September was warm and humid, and I lay on my bed in singlet and shorts, watching the lizards scuttle about on the walls. Then the door opened and Mulia entered the room.

'She had bathed, she had perfumed her hair, and she looked quite magnificent as she stood there before me, with the sun from the open window slanting across her great quivering breasts. She lay down beside me and began to caress and stroke my limbs almost as though she worshipped my body. And although you may not believe it now, my body once had all the attributes of the perfect male physique. I was slim-waisted like a pipal leaf, with fine broad shoulders; and my thighs were like plantains, long and smooth and powerful. That was—how many years ago—five, ten, I don't remember ... But it doesn't take long for a man to lose his vigour and freshness. Women and trees last longer.

'Anyway, to return to what I was saying, Mulia began caressing me, but I was totally unresponsive to her ministrations.

' "What is wrong?" she asked.

' "Nothing" I said. "I am unwell, that is all. I will be all right in a day or two."

'And I got up from the bed and went to the tap to refresh

myself with a cold bath.

'That evening I bathed in the river. I felt listless and ill at ease, and perhaps I was hoping that the icy water would instil new life in me. Thousands bathed daily in the river. Each person sought his own cure, his own solutions, his own personal benediction; and that surging mass of human flesh appeared to me as one living entity, a shapeless jelly of throbbing amoeba, struggling for life on the banks of a timeless river. Was I a distinct and sacred individual, or was I just a part of the quivering jelly that sought cohesion in the swirling waters? And did help come from within or from without? Did it come from the mind, as my teacher once said, or was there really a potency, a magic, in the waters of the river? Bathing should be a rite, not a routine, I thought.

'Mulia was worried about me. She made me one of her concoctions, a bitter brew of senna leaves, rose petals, pomegranate-bark and laburnum seeds. The result was diarrhoea.

'I placed more reliance on Samyukta. A few hours with her, I thought, and I would soon be myself again. I had spent too much time with older women, and I needed the challenge of someone my own age. Or so I tried to convince myself.'

∞∞∞

THIRTEEN
ஐ௸

'Since my return, I had seen Samyukta occasionally but had not found an opportunity to be alone with her. Then one day her mother decided to visit a fair on the other side of the river, and Samyukta, pleading a headache, remained at home. I found her combing her long black hair in front of the mirror. I knew that she spent many hours at the mirror, and suspected that she was deeply in love with her own beauty.

'I began kissing her on her lips and throat, and presently she got up and undressed and came to bed with me. She had blossomed in the past year, and I think there were few women who could match her physical attractions. She had never failed to rouse me, to meet my challenge. She was prepared to do so now—even eager to please—for in pleasing me, homage would be paid to her own beauty.

'But something terrible had happened to me. My failure with Mulia was not a thing of the moment. There I was, lying beside a girl with whom at one time I had been brutal in my lovemaking. And now, though there was no diminishing of desire, I found myself helpless, unable to take possession of her. For the first time in my life I found myself up against forces beyond my control. Fear crept over me. Had the woman of the hills completely destroyed my manhood? Or had my own body rebelled against me?

'The unfocussed stare of desire faded from Samyukta's eyes. She looked at me in surprise, and then in anger. My inadequacy was an insult to her beauty and womanhood. And she asked the same question that Mulia had asked: "What is wrong?"'

' "I don't know," I said. "I must be ill. Or it's the evil eye."

'She got up and began to dress. She said nothing. But her silence was more eloquent than speech.

' "I'll come again," I said, "When I feel better."

'How pathetic it sounded!

'And of course she said nothing. After all, what was there to say? A woman can hide her frigidity, but a man's impotence is obvious.'

'I primed myself on strong country liquor, and when evening came on and the sun sank in the river, and night crept up to cover our imperfections, I walked unsteadily towards the house with the green lantern and made my way upstairs. Shankhini's door was open. I walked in, but she was not to be seen anywhere. Feeling giddy and sick, I stumbled into the bathroom and, supporting myself against the sink, began retching. Then, exhausted, I leant back against the wall. And while I stood there trying to pull myself together, I heard the voices of two people who had entered the room.

'One voice was Shankhini's—I recognized it immediately. The other was a man's voice.

'They spoke together for a few minutes, then the bed creaked under their combined weight. I couldn't resist moving to the bathroom door and looking through the curtains. The bathroom was in darkness, but Shankhini's bedroom was brightly lit. She lay on her bed, a fragile figure, while her guest for the night took his pleasure.

'The man, a stranger in town, had close-cropped grey hair, hollow cheeks, and skinny legs; he must have been at least sixty. But he went about the whole business with all the verve and vigour of a young stallion.

'I watched in fear and fascination. Fear for myself, fascination at the old man. I had fancied myself the world's most accomplished lover. And there I stood, finished before

I was thirty, while a man who was more than twice my age performed wonders on a bed. My ego was shattered. My self-esteem lay in the washbasin.

'There was a door leading from the bathroom to the passageway and, unable to face Shankhini, I departed ignominiously, stumbling into the street and being sick again on the pavement.'

∞∞∞

FOURTEEN

ဆာ

The clear light of a September dawn has spread across the mountains, and from outside the cave comes the call of the whistling-thrush, a song sweet and haunting, recalling for me a different kind of joy. But inside the cave it is dark and clammy, a home for those who despise the light—bats, rodents and hollow men.

All the awe I had at first felt for the recluse disappeared at the very moment that the sun came shouting over the hills. There is nothing more beautiful than daylight. I want to flee from the cave, from all within it. Renunciation? He has not renounced the world, he has hidden from it. And I wonder how many thousands there are like him—men who have run, not simply from the world but from themselves; men who, hating themselves, cannot bear to see their own reflections in the faces of other men.

He has produced a small chillum—a clay pipe—and filled it with the dried leaves of the cannabis plant.

'No wonder you eat so little,' I say.

'It is mental food I require. Those few or many years ago, of which I have told you, when I thought that by strengthening my mental powers I might regain my manhood, I went again to the man who had taught me to concentrate, to bend others to my will. But he could do nothing for me. Perhaps he had lost his hypnotic powers in the same way that I had lost my physical powers—a failure of conservation!'

'And yet this weed which grows all about me, has made life tolerable. It has so solaced me that in my fantasies I can experience all those sensual pleasures without my miserable body having to do anything! Surely that's an achievement—

surely that's victory for mind over matter!'

'I wouldn't call it that,' I say, now ready to refute. 'If it's the plant that brings you mental ease, that makes it a victory of matter over mind. Surely the only victory comes when the mind is free.'

'Perhaps, perhaps. But nothing else, human or divine, could help me. I had only one talent, you know. Misuse a gift, and you destroy it. And when I lost mine, I turned my back on the world and all it stood for.'

'But the world isn't exclusively a place for the pursuit of sensual pleasure.'

'No. But I was a sensualist. There was nothing else I could pursue.'

Before I go, I ask him where I can find the woman who had stolen his manhood—the hill-woman who had overpowered him with her own much stronger sensuality.

'Why?' he asks. 'Do you wish to lose your manhood too?'

'No. I wish to regain it. Or rather, I wish to discover it. And only a woman who can give so much of herself can revive true passion in a man.'

'You are wrong. A woman of great passion can only diminish a man.'

'That is because you were in love with your ego, you were too concerned about your self-esteem. You took the love but spurned the lover. And so you had to lose both. I hope to find them yet ...'

And I leave him in the cave with his cold thoughts, and the cold ashes of his dead fire, and the cold corpse he still inhabits.

I leave my dead self in the cave and continue my search for the perfect stranger in the night.

❧❧

READ MORE IN PENGUIN

In every corner of the world, on every subject under the sun, Penguin represents quality and variety – the very best in publishing today.

For complete information about books available from Penguin – including Puffins, Penguin Classics and Arkana – and how to order them, write to us at the appropriate address below. Please note that for copyright reasons the selection of books varies from country to country.

In India: Please write to *Penguin Books India Pvt Ltd, 706 Eros Apartments, 56 Nehru Place, New Delhi, 110019*

In the United Kingdom: Please write to *Dept. JC, Penguin Books Ltd, Bath Road, Harmondsworth, West Drayton, Middlesex, UB7 ODA, UK*

In the United States: Please write to *Penguin USA Inc., 375 Hudson Street, New York, NY 10014*

In Canada: Please write to *Penguin Books Canada Ltd, 10 Alcorn Avenue, Suite 300, Toronto, Ontario M4V 3B2*

In Australia: Please write to *Penguin Books Australia Ltd, 487 Maroondah Highway, Ring Wood, Victoria 3134*

In New Zealand: Please write to *Penguin Books (NZ) Ltd, 182–190 Wairau Road, Private Bag, Takapuna, Auckland 9*

In the Netherlands: Please write to *Penguin Books Netherlands B.V., Keizersgracht 231 NL–1016 DV Amsterdam*

In Germany : Please write to *Penguin Books Deutschland GmbH, Metzlerstrasse 26, 60595 Frankfurt am Main, Germany*

In Spain: Please write to *Penguin Books S. A., Bravo Murillo, 19-1' B, E-28015 Madrid, Spain*

In Italy: Please write to *Penguin Italia s.r.l., Via Felice Casati 20, I–20124 Milano*

In France: Please write to *Penguin France S. A., 17 rue Lejeune, F–31000 Toulouse*

In Japan: Please write to *Penguin Books Japan, Ishikiribashi Building, 2-5-4, Suido, Tokyo 112*

In Greece: Please write to *Penguin Hellas Ltd, Dimocritou 3, GR–106 71 Athens*

In South Africa: Please write to *Longman Penguin Southern Africa (Pty) Ltd, Private Bag X08, Bertsham 2013*

OUR TREES STILL GROW IN DEHRA
Ruskin Bond

Semi-autobiographical in nature, these stories span the period from the author's childhood to the present. We are introduced, in a series of beautifully imagined and crafted cameos, to the author's family, friends, and various other people who left a lasting impression on him. In other stories we revisit Bond's beloved Garhwal hills and the small towns and villages that he has returned to time and time again in his fiction.

Together with his well-known novella, *A Flight of Pigeons* (which was made into the film *Junoon*), which also appears in this collection, these stories once again bring Ruskin Bond's India vividly to life.

TIME STOPS AT SHAMLI
Ruskin Bond

Ruskin Bond's characters—who live for the most part in the country's small towns and villages—are not the sort who make the headlines but are, none-theless, remarkable for their quiet heroism, their grace under pressure and the manner in which they continue to cleave to the old values: honesty, fidelity, a deep-rooted faith in God, family and their neighbour. They do have problems, of course—the sudden death of a loved parent, un-fulfilled dreams, natural calamities, ghostly visita-tions, a respected teacher gone crooked, strangers who make a nuisance of themselves in a town marooned in time—but these are solved with a minimum of fuss and tremendous dignity. Taken together these stories are a magnificent evocation of the real India by one of the country's foremost writers.

'An educative, charming and often memorable onetime read . . . .'

—*Sunday Observer*

'An enjoyable rustic trip back in time.'

—*Straits Times*

2-4-22
Katie
+ Gaskers'
Garden
93 Marathon
- 95
MT
Pam